Sky of Bliss

by

Alicia Fadgen

Published by Pen It Publications in the U.S.A.

812-371-4128 www.penitpublications.com

ISBN: 978-1-63984-272-8

Edited by Marla Williams VanHoy

CONTENTS

BLISS

supreme happiness, utter joy or contentment

CHAPTER 1
Overjoyed

I am going to beat you to the top!" I sprinted through the glittery sunflowers as sweat dripped from my brow. Sunbeams glistened off each petal. The sweet aroma filled my lungs. In the distance, stood a tall, colorful mountain. As I approached the slopes, the flower scent faded and was replaced with the smell of heaven. I leaped onto the mountain as my dirtied sneaker sunk like quicksand. Chocolate fudge wrapped around my ankle, slowing up my speed. My eyes focused in on the blue M&M, halfway submerged into vanilla scoops. I placed my left foot onto the candy and pulled my other foot free as I continued up the ice cream sundae. Trying my very best to not slip on the caramel dripping down, I used the rainbow jimmies to stay sturdy. The farther up I got, the more smells I experienced. Banana, chocolate, and vanilla surrounded me. Gummy bears and cookie dough were the best accents to speed me up.

"I will get to that cherry before you do!" Mom teased as I matched it with a pout. Competition ran through our veins, determined to win. We raced side by side until I felt Mom's warm arms wrap around me, pulling me to the ground as we landed into fluffy whipped cream. A cramp formed in my side from laughing uncontrollably. My fast-paced breathing started to slow down as I was blinded by headlights.

Quickly snapping back to reality, I saw my dad's truck pull into the driveway. "Dad's home! Think he will want ice cream sundaes for dinner?" I joked, hoping Mom would agree.

"After today's adventure, I could use an ice cream sundae," Mom replied, smirking.

I could tell from her eyes up in the clouds, she was trying her hardest to escape the daydream. This wasn't our first time running through glitter sunflowers up an ice cream sundae mountain or traveling to unknown worlds. Mom had the most extraordinary gift. She had the gift of imagination. Like magic, she could take my mind to the most amazing places.

One of my most favorite adventures was the time we dived under the purple sea to a world of unicorn mermaids. I also couldn't forget the bumpy ride along a pirate ship, as we searched for the rare pink gem. Hands down, my most exciting journey was to the portal waterfall. It could transport you to just about anywhere. Mom always said these imaginary adventures kept her young.

About five years ago, she encouraged me to invite my friends along. After introducing these imaginary adventures to a few of my closest neighbors, word spread like wildfire. Before I knew it, just about every kid from the neighborhood would jump off the bus on a Friday afternoon and meet on my lawn. Some came with dress up clothes, while others brought household items to transform. The excitement was undeniable, so the tradition continues on.

****

My name was Layla Lance. I was your average ten-year-old, a little short, but my outgoing personality made up for that. I tended to dress in bright colors since Mom insisted that it brought out my big blue eyes. I usually matched my hair Scrunchie with my choice of outfit. Scrunchies were my thing, considering my hair had a mind of its own. My golden-brown curls seemed to want to go on all kinds of adventures at the same time, in completely opposite directions. In other words, my hair was an untamed mess. For the ten years I had been on this planet, my life couldn't get better. I was an only child, which most people think is a disadvantage, but I never felt lonely. I was born and raised in a beautiful neighborhood surrounded by kids who were all my age. They were basically family, so no complaints there.

Now let's talk about my mom, Kristine. Some might look down on stay-at-home moms, but my life wouldn't be so wonderful if it wasn't for her being there at all times. She was my best friend, my comforter, my everything. Her heart was filled with so much fun, imagination, and kindness. She was the most selfless person I knew. She put everyone's needs above her own. When I was six, I broke my foot during gym class. Mom completely spoiled me during that first week. She was by my side the entire time, cooking my favorite dinners and helping me shower. She gave me so much attention, she disregarded herself. She went five days without a shower. Every time Dad would tell her to go freshen up, she would not leave me. It wasn't until I asked her to go get a shower due to not wanting to smell her any longer, she laughed and agreed. It was just one of many moments where she put my concerns above her own. She always smothered me with love. Not only was she an angel of a person, but she was stunning. Her jet-black hair perfectly complemented her big, bold, blue eyes. I was lucky she passed those eyes down to me.

Speaking of good traits being passed down, Dad blessed me with hard-work ethic. My dad, Henry, was as hard-working as they came. His wardrobe consisted of work shirts and oil-filled pants, but that didn't take away from his infectious smile. He worked two jobs to be able to provide for our family. Whenever Dad had free time, he always made sure that we went on real adventures. Last year, we set out on a camping trip. I caught my first fish, a bass worth keeping. He was so proud and had Mom take a picture. He had it framed and had it sitting on our mantel above the fireplace. As proud as he was of me, I was equally as proud to be his daughter. His strength and love for our family was unmatchable. I was definitely a daddy's girl, and I wouldn't have had it any other way.

"Dad, any chance you may want an ice cream sundae for dinner?"

"I thought you'd never ask," Dad replied, smiling.

We scurried around the kitchen grabbing every flavor ice cream from the fridge, sprinkles, syrup, whipped cream from the cabinet and even brownies that Mom and I had baked that afternoon, to make the most delicious dessert. Mom cleared the table as I licked the bowl to get every last drop of my strawberry ice cream.

"Hey, squirt, grab the popcorn." Dad pointed me in the direction of the kitchen as he grabbed our favorite movie off the shelf and placed it into the DVD player.

As I rushed from the room, Mom grabbed a soft, oversized blanket.

Flashing across the TV screen read the movie's title, *It's A Wonderful Life*.

I always think of Dad as George Bailey, someone who was there to help everyone above himself. It didn't matter what time of day it was, if someone had a broken appliance, or a sudden loss of air conditioning, he was at their doorstep moments later. I selfishly hated that. I wanted all of Dad's free time. Why should he have to work after work hours were over? But all of his explanations showed his caring heart.

"Mrs. Smith has a newborn baby, and with this cold winter night, the baby is going to need heat," he would explain. Then my selfish mind would sit in awe. He was always right. He always looked at the bigger picture and helped those who needed it most.

Jumping between my parents, I grabbed a handful of popcorn from the bowl. The butter gathered on my lips, as my tongue made sure not to miss an ounce of it. The three of us cuddled closely, as tears streamed down our cheeks.

Clarence's note to George was such a valuable lesson: *Remember, no man is a failure who has friends.* This part of the movie always got us emotional. The family and friends surrounded George as he squeezed them tightly, embracing his wonderful life. *Hark! The Herald Angels Sing* filled the room, as everyone came together to show their appreciation for George Bailey and his family. My tears didn't really come from the movie, but from my love for Dad and Mom. They continuously teach me to live a humble life, and I am so grateful for them and our wonderful life.

The night was coming to an end. My mouth let out a yawn as salt formed in my eyes. I rested my head on Dad's shoulder. Mom leaned in on me, nestling me in. Pure happiness filled my heart as we all drifted off.

"Dad, do you have to work on Saturdays? All of my friends get to have both of their parents home on the weekends." My selfish ways of thinking came back full force. I just loved every second I get with both Mom and Dad, and I wanted more of it.

"I wish, sweetheart. You know I only work this hard so that I can give you everything you deserve. You love our house, right?"

"Yes, Dad."

"Well then, I must work so we can stay here forever." He ruffled my hair, making it crazier than it already was. "I promise when I get home, we will make a nice bonfire out back."

Dad always knew the way to my heart—and my stomach.

"S'mores included?"

"Of course!"

"I love you, Dad!"

"I love you, sweetie." Dad squatted down and kissed me goodbye. Standing up, he leaned down to kiss Mom. As great as their love was, I could go without seeing that. Gross.

"I love you too. Be careful and have a great day." Mom's face could never hide her feelings. She was just as sad to see Dad leave as I was. She waved him goodbye and blew him a kiss. Dad quickly reached his hand out and grabbed it. Now, that kind of kiss is more acceptable. To cheer Mom up, I knew just the thing.

"Mom, can I have a few friends over today? Savannah, Johnny, and I never finished our under the sea adventure." Last Friday, we were in the middle of looking for the buried treasure when a storm hit. Our adventure had quickly come to a halt.

"Yes, you can. I'll make some seafood for lunch."

"Yuck!! Maybe just some Goldfish to snack on."

Mom laughed. "You've got it!"

Johnny ran around his lawn, practicing his speed for football. He was my neighbor across the street. Our houses were so close, we could basically see in each other's windows. Johnny was my age and was born and raised here as well. He was kind of like my twin brother, even had matching curls. Johnny was not shy. He was actually too talkative, always getting in trouble in school for chatting. But he was a really great friend. He came off super tough, making sure to remain dirty at all times and join every sports team. Behind closed doors, he was actually a softy at heart. One time, we were watching *Sandlot*. At the end of the movie, a large fence fell on the Saint Bernard. My tough friend Johnny cried enough tears to fill the ocean. He was also super thoughtful, saving me a spot on the bus every day. Most people teased him, saying he had a crush on me, but I knew the truth. He was just a really loyal friend.

"Hey, Johnny! Take a break from football and help me find this treasure," I yelled over. He quickly turned to look at me, smiled, and dropped the football.

"Be right there," he yelled back.

As I waited for Johnny to make his way over, I looked to my left. Savannah's house sat directly next to mine. Although she was my next-door neighbor, there was a little bit more land between our houses. Savannah is nine-years-old. Even though she was a year younger, she was my absolute best friend. We were so alike, our parents joked that we were separated at birth. She was even the same height as I was and had the same golden-brown hair, except hers was super straight. She usually always wore her hair in a braid and accessorized it with a bow. Savannah was a little bit more on the shy side, but if you messed with her friends, she would definitely speak up.

We went to summer camp together two years ago. Unfortunately, we didn't get to bunk together. I was stuck bunking with this awful girl named Riley. She made my camping experience horrible. She put lotion on my toothbrush, locked me out of the cabin numerous times, and called me Loser Layla. When I cried to Savannah about it, she didn't even hesitate. She came up with a master plan. She decided to write a nasty note to the camp advisor and sign it from Riley. It didn't go over well for her. When Riley denied the letter, several girls came forward, admitting she had also been rude to them. She was kicked out of camp the following day. With an angry look on her face, she pushed past me and Savannah with luggage in hand. Savannah's shyness quickly faded as she called out, "So long, Rude Riley!" From that day, I knew Savannah would always have my back.

I could hear Savannah's bike bell ringing but couldn't see her yet. I looked a little farther up, and there she was, riding her bike my way. I waved my arms in the air to get her attention. Her momentum picked up, and she got to me even quicker than Johnny did.

"Hey, bestie." Savannah smiled.

"Are you ready to find this treasure?" The weather was beautiful; nothing could stand in our way. Savannah nodded as Johnny joined us on the sidewalk. We all ran to my backyard together.

I grabbed a shovel out of my shed. Sitting on the ground next to it, was Savannah's bucket. She had left it there from last Friday, after the storm had hit. I grabbed it out and handed it to her.

"Okay, Johnny, are you ready to be the dolphin again?"

"Flipper is here, reporting for duty," Johnny said with a salute. He put his hands down to his side, feet together, and leaped in the air. He was always super silly.

"Mermaid Sparkle is ready to dig under those shells," Savannah squealed.

Savannah loved mermaids. Her bedroom was painted ocean blue, and her comforter had a large, sequined mermaid on it. I also loved mermaids, but I settled for being the starfish. My parents always reminded me to think of ways to make others happy. I stuck my arms out wide and extended both my legs. It looked more like I was doing jumping jacks. My neon-colored shirt helped me feel more like a tropical rainbow starfish. I loved all things tropical. Mom always called me a beach babe, since I was born in the summer. Last summer, we went on vacation to the Bahamas. It was like a dream. I never saw such beautiful, clear water. The sand sparkled and the sun warmed my soul. There were also lots of starfish, which reminded me, back to digging.

Savannah, Johnny, and I spent about thirty minutes last Friday trying to find a treasure Mom had buried. The imaginary game started as three sea creatures looking for a treasure that could turn us into humans. When Mom found out about this adventure, she couldn't help herself. She had us close our eyes as she buried a treasure in my backyard. Due to the unfortunate weather, we had to put our treasure hunt on hold. Thank goodness today was beautiful. It was seventy degrees out and not a cloud in the sky.

"Layla, do you really think your mom buried a treasure?" Johnny was starting to believe we were digging for nothing.

After an hour of digging, I started to feel exhausted myself. But I knew Mom. There was definitely a treasure; she was just really good at hiding things.

"Of course, she did! She takes our imagination games very seriously."

We all giggled, knowing I was right. There was one time when Mom had us search the house for a hidden cave. We looked for an entire hour, which felt like days. We started to think she was tricking us, until she pointed out the hidden steps leading to the attic. It was a string that hung from the ceiling. Although I knew it led to the attic, I never went up there. It was an area for storage, and I never thought Mom would clear it out for our adventure. We slowly walked up those wooden steps to see the most magical cave. Mom had a blanket fort that stretched across the length of the attic. She used the storage boxes to keep it up and put Christmas lights inside. She also had snacks and books set up for us. We spent the rest of our day up there. It was one of my favorite days.

"Yes! Your mom's famous lemonade!" Johnny yelled over to me.

Sitting on the picnic table, was a big pitcher of pink lemonade and a treasure chest bowl filled with Goldfish. *Mom is the best.* She must have snuck it out here while we were busy digging. We all could use a snack break. Savannah and I ran over to the table to join Johnny.

"Mermaids and starfish don't eat fish, so looks like this is all for me," Johnny joked.

"Nice try," smirked Savannah.

As we sat filling our bellies, I couldn't help but smell the delicious feast taking place inside. The picnic table sat right outside my kitchen window. Mom was cooking up some homemade mashed potatoes and steak. That was Dad's favorite meal. Mom started a tradition from as far as I could remember. Every Saturday, she cooked Dad's favorite meal and set up board games on the living room table. After Dad got home from work, we filled our faces and then spent the night playing games and sharing laughs. She called it Fun Family Saturday.

"Are you sure we checked under the tree?" asked Savannah.

Johnny smacked his hands together to get the sand off.

"Yes! We looked there twice now."

I looked around the yard to see what area we could attempt next. "Maybe we can dig under the picnic bench?"

"Or under the swings," Savannah chimed in.

"Or by that tire," Johnny offered.

Undecided on where to go next, I suggested, "Let's all split up and dig; that will help us find the treasure quicker."

The others agreed, and we immediately separated, beginning to dig in our own areas. While we searched, Savannah continuously brushed through her "mermaid" hair and Johnny lay on his belly while he flipped his tail. They both were really getting into their characters. It was much too awkward for me to keep my star stance while digging, so I gave up pretty quickly when it came down to my character.

With only ten minutes back into digging, Johnny threw down the stick he had been digging with. "I think I've got something." He jumped up and down in excitement.

Savannah and I ran, hoping to feast our eyes on the treasure. Glistening in the sun, something beautiful sat below the dirt.

Johnny slowly loosened it to find out it was just an old rock. "Aw, man! I thought I had it." He sat back, crossing his arms in disappointment.

We tried to comfort him as we patted him on the back.

The sun slowly started to lower as the sky became a beautiful, pale orange.

"Let's continue this treasure hunt tomorrow. I need to start setting up for my bonfire." I was eager for the bonfire that night. Dad always told the greatest stories as we gazed at the fire. Mom always laughed at his silliness. He usually told stories from his day at work, which involved his clumsiness. But Mom laughed the most at his childhood stories. One time, he told us about his newfound talent. When he was my age, he decided to try picking up rocks with his feet. Don't ask me why. Mom already started to chuckle when she heard that. He said he picked them up with his toes and launched them as far as he could. One day, he was trying to launch a rock and it flew sideways and into his neighbor's sliding glass door. He lived in an apartment complex and the neighbor sat below him. As soon as he heard a shatter, he took off up the stairs and into his apartment. Moments later, there was a knock on his door. He was so afraid of getting into trouble, he hid in his room and made his mom get the door. She came into his room and demanded he face his neighbor. With sweaty palms and knots in his stomach, he approached the door.

"I believe my cat knocked over your planter, and I wanted to apologize. I know you made that in school," said Betty, from downstairs.

Dad couldn't believe it. The rock he had thrown didn't shatter her window. It shattered his planter. And Betty thought it was her cat. He explained to her what happened after he realized it wasn't her window. Mom and I laughed so hard that night.

✳✳✳✳

Johnny wiped the sweat dripping from his forehead.

"Aw, man, I got sand in my eye," he complained.

He took his shirt and wiped away until he was able to see clearly. Savannah dusted off her knees, trying to keep herself as clean as possible. We were all tired from the steady digging.

"Bye, guys! See you tomorrow." I waved before making my way inside.

"Hey, Lay, any luck finding the treasure?" Mom asked.

"Not yet; we are going to try again tomorrow." I was a little disappointed. This adventure was lasting much longer than the others, and I just wanted to see what Mom had buried. But it also gave me more fun with my two best friends.

"Okay, honey, go wash up before Dad gets home, then dinner, games, and bonfire time! Woot woot!" Mom danced around.

I smiled as I turned to race upstairs to get ready for a fun family night.

"I wanna know, have you ever seen the rain?" I could hear Mom downstairs belting out Creedence Clearwater Revival. I joined her, spinning around, as we set the table. The clock ticked, as my eyes stayed glued to it. Dad was running a tad late.

Knock, knock. Who could be knocking at this time? Did Savannah forget her bucket again?

Mom danced her way over to the door as I continued setting the table.

"Are you Mrs. Lance?"

"I am. Is everything okay?"

I peeked my head around the corner to see two police officers at my door. My stomach instantly dropped.

The officer anxiously wiped his hands on his pants. "There has been an accident."

The plate from my hand dropped to the floor, shattering into a million pieces.

CHAPTER 2
Devastated

Mrs. Lance, your husband has been in an accident. Unfortunately, he did not survive the crash."

The shattered plate represented my heart. *I must be asleep. This has to be a nightmare. Wake up! Wake up!*

"We are so sorry. If there is anything we can do, please don't hesitate to call us," sympathized the officers as they nodded their heads and walked away.

The red and blue lights flashed in my eyes as my head started to ache. It felt like a rock concert was pounding in my brain. Mom turned around with tears in her eyes. When she realized I heard, she ran to my side. My body went limp as she caught me.

"Noooooo!" I screamed. The pain was so sharp, a feeling I had never felt in my life. It was excruciating. The tears streamed down my cheeks and onto Mom's shoulder. Her tears soaked my shirt. We did not know what else to do but to squeeze one another and cry. Life would never be the same. We sat, cradled on the kitchen floor, as the devastation took us into a slumber.

****

One month later...

Uhh. My curtain slipped off my window, as I was blinded by the sun. I would have to remember to ask Mom for black-out shades. Or maybe I should permanently move my bedroom up to the attic. I was not ready to face the outside world. I wasn't even ready to face the hallway. A piece of me was gone forever. How was I supposed to function without that piece? I wanted Dad here.

"Sweetheart, you have some company. Johnny and Savannah want to see if you would like to play outside." I was not interested at all.

"Tell them I am sleeping," I responded.

Unfortunately, Mom couldn't get the hint. She slowly creaked open my door.

"I think some sun and treasure hunting may be good for you." She was trying really hard, but I was not ready.

"I am not in the mood today," I sighed. "Any luck finding a job?"

"Not yet, sweetie. Being a stay-at-home mother hasn't been helpful on my resumes. But don't worry, I will find something."

The days continued on. They grew longer and longer. I remained inside. I spent most of my time writing in my journal. I was having a hard time talking with Mom. I didn't want to upset her by talking about Dad. She suggested I write my feelings down. She bought me a mermaid journal. It did seem to be helping. One thing that probably wasn't helping was my addiction to watching *It's A Wonderful Life* on repeat. I couldn't help it. For a small moment, I felt like Dad was watching it with me. I seemed to cry even more as I watched it alone, realizing my life was no longer wonderful.

"Dad, I think I got something!" I yelled, as I tried my hardest to reel in my line.

"You've got this, squirt!" Dad wrapped his arms around me and grabbed onto the pole. We both pulled with all our strength.

"This is a really big one." Dad started to sweat as we tugged harder and harder.

A large fin started to appear above the surface. My heart sank into my stomach as I laid my eyes on a great white shark.

"Ahhhhhhhhh!!!!!!"

"Help! Help!" my mom shouted.

I lunged forward in my bed and woke out of my sleep. It was just a nightmare. A nightmare that I wish I could have stayed in for just a moment longer. I could put up with being shark bait just to have another second with Dad.

"Help!" Mom shouted. I was no longer asleep. Mom needed me!

Her voice was so faint. It had to be coming from outside. I grabbed my sandals and headed out the back door.

"Mom! Mom!" My chest tightened and my legs felt weak. I had already lost Dad. I couldn't lose Mom. I quickly looked side to side as my hands began dripping sweat. My heart raced. Mom was hunched over by the swing set. I leaped across the garden, the seesaw, and made it to her.

I fell to my knees as I placed my hand on Mom's back.

"What happened? Are you okay?"

"No! I can't escape the forest monster! His weeds are wrapped around me! You must cut me loose so we can get to the cave. The hidden gem is inside!"

I couldn't believe it. I quickly felt annoyed as I rolled my eyes. Mom knew I didn't want to join any imaginary games. The neighborhood kids had knocked on my door every Friday for the past three months. My answer had been no and would remain no. As much as I would love to escape reality, I couldn't. Dad was gone forever.

"Mom! You scared me! I am not in the mood for an imaginary adventure."

Crack. Boom. Thunder filled the air.

"Layla, you are making the forest monster mad," Mom warned.

She needs to give up. I will not be saving her from some stupid forest monster.

Within seconds, rain poured down.

"You hurt his feelings, and now he is crying," Mom joked.

As much as I wanted to ignore her silly ways, I couldn't hold back any longer. It seemed like nature was helping her out. I let out a laugh.

"Dad would have wanted this. He would want you to be a kid again, having fun outside." Mom had tears in her eyes. I could tell in that moment, she needed me as much as I needed her. She just wanted to see me smile again. I knew, deep down, she was right. Dad would have wanted me to join her. I decided to give it a shot.

"Okay, I cut you loose. Now, where do we go?"

"To the tree house! I mean the cave!" Mom yelled as she grabbed my hand. We climbed up the ladder to shelter ourselves from the rain.

"Thanks, Mom."

"For what?"

"For forcing me out of the house."

Mom put her arm around me. We sat there soaking wet as we watched the storm. I couldn't help but feel like the storm was my current situation. I was drowning in sadness. But maybe one day, a rainbow would come out of this. For now, I would just take in this moment with Mom.

****

"Layla, are you really sure your mom buried a treasure?" asked Johnny.

"Yes, Johnny. Maybe we just need to dig deeper."

Three months had passed, and I decided I needed a little normalcy in my life. I agreed to continue the treasure hunt with Johnny and Savannah.

Savannah brought over cupcakes. She knew me all too well. Cupcakes were my favorite dessert. She even decorated them with sprinkles, using my favorite color, purple. Johnny brought popsicles. We had a little picnic outside, then decided to dig under the treehouse. With an hour of digging and no luck, we needed a break.

I placed a quilt on the ground, and we lay on our backs staring up at the clouds. I couldn't help but think of Dad.

"I think it is time we bring another blanket," I said to Dad as I held up the quilt.

"Your mom worked very hard on making that. Who cares if it has seen better days. It makes me feel like Mom is on the trip with us." Dad smiled.

"You are right. I will have her sew up the holes." I continued to pack up the truck. We were headed on a camping trip, a few miles from the house. Although we would be close to home, Dad loved having a piece of Mom on our Father/Daughter trips. He really loved her.

"Did you hear me?" Savannah's face was about five centimeters away from mine.

"I am so sorry. I must have been daydreaming," I apologized.

"I said, we have really missed you." Savannah smiled.

"Yeah, we have been so bored without you. Adventures aren't the same," said Johnny.

"I know. I have missed you, too."

I pulled them in for a hug.

"Did you kids want to join us for dinner? It's spaghetti night," Mom called out. With no hesitation and growling bellies, we made our way inside. It was a really good day. Until it wasn't.

It was close to midnight and I woke from my sleep. I could hear crying. I followed the sound to Mom's room. I gently pressed my ear to the door. I could hear Mom sobbing as she spoke out to Dad. She begged him for strength. She asked him for guidance. Through her tears, she expressed her fears about losing the house, because she couldn't find a job.

We couldn't lose our house. My heart sank into my stomach. I headed back to bed and cried myself to sleep.

Ring. Ring. The phone rang. I picked up the wireless phone that sat by my bedside. I could hear two voices, Gram and Mom.

Mom must have picked up the phone in the kitchen. I sat in silence, as I decided to listen in on their call.

"Hi, hon. How are you and my beautiful granddaughter making out?"

"We have good days and bad. But I am really worried, Mom," expressed Mom.

"I wish I wasn't in this retirement home, or else you would be living with me," Gram said.

"I know, Mom, and I really appreciate it. I'm just really worried because I haven't had any luck finding a job, and the bills are no longer being paid. I received a letter the other day that our house will be going into foreclosure soon. I haven't had the heart to tell Layla."

Chunks formed in my throat. As much as I wanted to hang up, I needed to hear more.

"Oh, Kristine. I wish I could help you."

"Mom, I know you do. Your health and home are what you need to worry about, not me. You have done plenty for us over all these years. I will figure something out. I just need to find a job. That should help us get back on our feet."

" I have the perfect idea! You know your great-grandmother, Pearl?"

"I mean, I remember stories about her. The hardest working female in the family."

"She sure was. She ran the most successful farm in her town. The farm is yours if you want it."

Farm? There was no way I was moving to a farm. This conversation kept getting worse. I didn't know how much more I could listen to.

"What? Are you okay, Mom?" My mom sounded confused.

"Her home and farm were left to my mother, your grandmother. Our family lived states away and didn't need the home. So, my mother passed it along to me. I never wanted to move away, so the house remains vacant. It is in a small town in Alabama."

"Alabama? Mother, that is hours from here."

"I understand, but what other options do you have? The town has several stores that I am sure would hire you, especially if they know who your great-grandmother was. She was well-known, always supplying the best fruits and vegetables. The house needs fixing up, but you will have plenty of time to do that. And maybe one day, you can restore the farmland."

"Mom, I wouldn't know the first thing about a farm, and how can I be that far away from you? How can I take Layla away from her friends?"

"Listen, you fix it up, and I'll move in with you. Layla is young. She will make new friends. Small towns are nice and friendly. She will love it."

"As long as you promise to move in when I am all done remodeling, I will do it."

"Wonderful. Change will be good for you guys."

I couldn't believe what I was hearing. Mom had actually agreed to this awful idea. I couldn't hold it in any longer.

"Alabama? A farm? There is no way! I will never leave my home!" I hung up the phone and threw my face into the pillow. I could hear Mom running up the steps. She threw the door open and ran to my side.

"Layla, that was not how I wanted you to find out. I am so sorry. I am trying my best. It looks like this is our only option." She placed her hand on my shoulder, which I quickly smacked away.

"You need to try harder! I can't move away from my friends. I can't leave Dad!" My eyes puffed up from the endless tears. This was the only home I had ever known. Every great memory with Dad was made here. I couldn't imagine leaving that all behind.

"Just because we leave this house, doesn't mean Dad won't always be in your heart. I think it will be a good change for us. We can create new memories. You are also very friendly. You will make friends wherever we go. And I promise, we can always come back and visit."

No matter what Mom said, I couldn't shake how I was feeling. The rainbow I had longed for didn't seem anywhere in sight. Instead, a black cloud continued to pour over me. I had no words. Mom sat for a moment longer, brushing through my hair. She then kissed my head and exited the room. I continued to lie in bed, staring at a picture of Savannah, Johnny, and myself. Savannah had gifted me the picture in a mosaic frame for my birthday last year. I didn't want to leave them. Life was not fair.

CHAPTER 3
Dread

A week had passed, and the arguments continued. Mom took over my packing, due to me being stubborn. Today, would be our final day here. I couldn't bear leaving my friends and my home.

"I can't go. We never even found the treasure," I yelled through my closed door, blocking Mom from seeing me.

"I will go dig it up right now."

"No. There is no fun in that. This just isn't fair." I crossed my arms and stomped my feet. I wasn't ready to back down.

"I know it's not, sweetheart. None of this is fair, but we need to overcome these obstacles together. Adventure has always been fun for us. This will be an amazing adventure."

I could hear the desperation in Mom's voice. I realized my door wasn't to block her from seeing me. It was to block me from seeing her. I finally opened my bedroom door. Mom was quickly wiping away tears. I still wasn't ready to fully give in, but I figured I would help pack. I grabbed an empty box that was sitting in the hallway. I didn't even make eye contact with Mom. I went straight back to my room and closed the door.

"I'll be downstairs if you need me."

I started with my closet. I really needed to learn some more organizational skills. What a mess. A shoebox sat in the corner with an inch of dust on top. I went to go toss it, until I heard something shake inside. I lifted the lid and was shocked to see what was inside. Inside, was a collection of memories shared between Dad and me. Movie tickets, random pictures, birthday and Father's Day cards I had given him over the years, and more, all tucked away in this box. I had no idea this box even existed. Dad was seriously the most thoughtful person. Maybe I was meant to find this. Maybe it was his way of showing how I could take our memories with me. I carefully placed the shoebox in with my other belongings, trying to stay optimistic.

Hours of packing went by. I was starting to feel exhausted. Mom peeked her head around my door. "How did you make out, sweetie? Do you need any help?"

I placed tape over the last box. "I'm good, Mom. I just wish Dad was here."

"I know. It has been a rough time for us, but I promise we will turn this farm and house into our very own. Let's get going so we can get on the road. Your friends are waiting to say goodbye."

This was the moment I had dreaded. I dragged my feet and made my way out the front door. "Goodbye, house, I will miss you." I paused as my eyes burned. "Goodbye, Dad."

"Goodbye, Dad?" Mom whispered. "Honey, Dad will be going on this adventure with us. I promise."

Maybe Mom was right. I did find a box full of memories.

I lifted my droopy head to see every neighborhood kid out front. They ran to me the second I walked out and tackled me to the ground.

"We love you, Layla! We will miss you so much!" They all smothered me with hugs. I felt a little claustrophobic but very loved.

"I will miss you guys so much!"

"Layla will be back real soon to visit. Don't worry." Mom knew my friends were feeling just as upset as I was. We all had tears piling up in our eyes.

"If you need anything at all, no matter the distance, we are all here for you and Layla." Savannah's mom hugged mine. They had gotten just as close as Savannah and I had. It made me realize that she would be losing her best friends as well.

"Thank you all so much for being the best neighbors, but most importantly, the best friends. I promise to come back to visit. We love you guys." Mom strained a smile and waved goodbye. Her eyes started to well up with tears.

I closed my door and stared out the back window as we pulled away. I wanted to take a mental picture one last time. My friends stood waving, some crying. Their parents embraced them with hugs. I glanced over at my house. A reflection of Dad stood in the doorway. *Goodbye, Dad.* A tear slowly rolled down my cheek.

"Ninety-nine bottles of beer on the wall, ninety-nine bottles of beer, take one down, pass it around, ninety-eight bottles of beer on the wall," sang Mom as she tried to lighten the mood in the car.

"Oh God, Mom. Please, no singing. It's already been an hour and my head can't take eleven more hours of that."

Mom chuckled. "Okay, so do you want to play a game? Maybe a little I-Spy?"

"I am just going to rest my eyes and try to get some sleep," I muttered.

"Good idea, sweetie. We will be there before you know it."

Another hour down, and farmland became more frequent.

Beep. Beep.

Distracted, Mom forgot to fill the gas tank. She was driving Dad's truck, a truck she had never driven before. The day Dad was in the accident, he had driven Mom's car. He told her he would take it to the car wash after work. He always went out of his way for Mom.

Thankfully, most of our stuff had fit. He had a big second cab, where I sat with boxes surrounding me. The rest of our items were tucked into the bed of the truck. Mom quickly grabbed her cellphone from the cup holder. She searched *gas stations near me.* To her luck, she would hit a gas station within ten miles.

"Yes! Here it is!" she yelled. I jolted up, half asleep.

"Mom! What... why are you screaming?"

"I am so sorry. I just needed to get gas. Go back to sleep." Little did she know, I never fully fell asleep, mostly pretended, so I didn't have to play any road trip games. My mind was racing, but I figured I should get some sleep. I closed my eyes, trying my best.

Mom hopped out of the truck and realized she'd pulled up on the wrong side. She jumped back in and swung around so she could actually fill the tank.

Ten minutes up the road, the truck started to smoke. Mom pulled over to the side in a complete panic. She couldn't imagine what was going on.

"Mom, what is wrong with the truck?"

"I have no idea. Let's get out."

We both quickly jumped out and Mom pulled her cellphone out to call a car service. "Oh, great. No service. Of course, I have no service because we're in the middle of nowhere!" She took a deep breath, pasting a smile on. "We are only ten minutes up the road from the gas station. We are going to have to walk back for some assistance."

"Great." I rolled my eyes in frustration.

The sun beating down made for an uncomfortable walk. The silence added to the tension. I just really didn't know what to say. Sweat dripped down my nose.

We finally made it back. "Can I have money for a drink? I am so thirsty."

"Of course, hon." Mom handed over a dollar and I made my way to the vending machine. I was only a short distance away, with my ears opened.

"Ma'am, what did you fill your truck with?" asked the gas station attendant.

"What do you mean, what did I fill it with? Gas, of course."

"Did you use diesel?"

"Ummm... no?"

"Ma'am, I am the mechanic here. I am sorry to say, but it looks like you're going to have a little bit of an issue with your engine."

"As in you can fix it for me? Or that I am unable now to drive my vehicle?"

"Well, unless you have the time and money, you can probably fix it with a new fuel system. Anywhere from three hundred to a thousand dollars should do the job."

"What?" Mom clearly looked upset as she shook her head. "You are kidding, right?" The attendant sat in silence, as Mom's shoulders drooped. "I don't have the time or money for this.

Do you, by chance, have a vehicle we can drive or a phone I can use?"

"I have a phone, ma'am."

Mom took the outstretched phone and thanked him before dialing the car service. I quickly grabbed my Cherry Coke and ran to Mom's side. She did not look happy.

"Layla, let's make our way back to the truck." We walked in silence once again. Mom instructed me to start unpacking the vehicle. Due to listening in on their conversation, I did not need to ask any questions. I started to grab boxes off the back seat. They were heavy, and I was hot. This felt like a bad omen. We were not meant to move. Now I wished I had gotten some shut-eye. I was exhausted, weak, and not in a good mood. Mom was in the back of the truck, yanking at the boxes. I heard her slip a few curse words. She might have been more frustrated than I was. Without speaking to one another, we yanked every item from the truck.

Mom and I waited for our rental car. We sat on top of the boxes, with drenched backs. After what felt like a lifetime, a tow truck pulled up to our rescue with a small, older car on the back of it. Mom's jaw dropped to the ground. Her aggravated expression soon turned to worried.

"Layla, whatever you don't mind leaving behind, put it back in the truck."

"What do you mean, Mom? You have to be kidding me."

"I wish I was. It won't all fit."

"And just when I thought things couldn't get worse."

There was no way I was going through all of those boxes. I didn't even care what I brought at this point. I threw box after box back into the truck. I was in a fit of rage. Things continued to go wrong. After stubbing my toe on the truck tire, I was done. I couldn't even help Mom finish packing the car. I sat in the back seat with my arms crossed, as my temples pulsed. Mom shoved box after box into the trunk, trying to fit as much as she could.

"As soon as I get settled, I will send over a check to have this fixed," Mom told the tow driver. She aimlessly watched Dad's truck go off into the horizon.

"This car smells! How did you not know what type of gas to put into the truck?"

"Layla, please just try to stay positive. I know this has been a nightmare so far, but there is nothing we can do to change our situation, not right now at least."

"I am going to sleep." I had hoped this really was all a nightmare, and maybe I would wake up, back home, next to Dad.

Miles felt longer and longer, and there was not a person in sight. I slowly opened my eyes, hoping to be tucked in my nice, warm bed. Unfortunately, I was still in the back of a smelly old car. I peered out the window as the sun started to set. Mom's window let in a gust of wind, as I smelled a musky, fresh scent. The cicadas buzzed and clicked. The sky was filled with shades of purple and pink. It was beautiful and peaceful.

"Layla, wake up. We are pulling up." The car bumped up and down as we made our way down a narrow dirt road. The land was wild, overgrown with tall weeds for miles. Sitting farther back on the property, was a tall, paint-chipped house.

You have got to be kidding me.

"Oh my," Mom whispered, thinking I couldn't hear her. We looked at the broken-down house that sat in front of us with no windows, holes in the porch, and cobwebs everywhere.

"This has to be a joke." Once again, things continued to go wrong.

"Let's look at this as a half-full cup. We could be homeless."

We crept to the door and opened it to darkness. A musty smell overwhelmed us. Mom clicked on the flashlight from her cellphone. The dim light was enough to see that we were upon a huge mess. Tapping on the ground, brought our attention downward to see a filthy rat with its long tail scurry across our feet.

"Ahhhhhhhhhh!!!!" We both screamed.

"What was that?"

We looked at each other and broke out into laughter. We couldn't compose ourselves. Tears streamed down our cheeks. We laughed on and on and on. Laughter seemed like the most reasonable response at this point.

"Tomorrow is a new day. Let's just call it a night, and we will head into town tomorrow."

"Sounds good, Mom."

We made our way to the backyard. A rusted fire pit sat in the middle of the field. It instantly made me think of the beloved bonfires I had shared with Dad. Maybe he was looking over us. Maybe this could be the sign I needed. We sat down next to one another and took in the silence, staring up at the sky. As alone as we were, a feeling of comfort overcame me. I smiled and rested my head on Mom's shoulder. Tomorrow would hopefully be a better day.

CHAPTER 4
Optimistic

Kinks formed in my back. The throw blankets gave little to no comfort, while lying on old, wooden baseboards.

"Mom, why didn't we sleep in the car last night? It would have been more comfortable than this old, dirty, broken, no-good floor!"

"Touché," Mom retorted. "We have enough money tucked away to get appliances, furniture, and food for the next several months. We will head to town and fill our bellies, then we will go shopping!"

Mom spent the car ride filling me in on the town. Gram had told her all about it, stories that had been passed down. She said the town had changed barely at all. Every store and eatery sat on one long street. The rest of the town was mainly farmland.

"That was fast," Mom said, pulling into town. It was a four-minute drive for us. As excited as I was to be getting away from the mess of our new home, my optimism quickly faded. A bunch of small shops lined the street. The sidewalks had cracks, and the signs were faded and rusty. *Welcome to Elkville* was painted across a chipped wood pallet.

"Elkville is a very small town with a population of around four-hundred-fifty people." Mom pretended to be a tour guide as I rolled my eyes. How was I going to make any friends with such a small amount of people? It seemed everyone knew each other, because we stuck out. Eyes became glued to us, as heads quickly turned our way. I skimmed the street looking for kids my age. So far, there were none. My belly started to moan. I didn't know if it was just as angry as I was, or if it needed to be fed.

"Mom, I am starving. Can we eat first?"

"Of course, sweetie."

We entered The Rooster Café. It was a seat yourself, so we grabbed a booth by the door. I will say, I was a fan of the color choice. Everything was lavender. It appeared to be old-fashioned, but still my favorite color. The place was pretty packed, as people continued to stare our way.

"Good morning, y'all, my name is Nancy. What can I get y'all?" a friendly waitress greeted us at the door. Mom was too busy, wide-eyed and glowing. Her eyes followed the perimeter of the diner, smiling at all of the antiques. Back home, we had one antique store that was forty-five minutes away. She drove there once a week. She never bought a thing. She just loved to look at all the old antiques. I never understood why she loved all that old stuff. Dad never understood why she wasted so much gas just to look at stuff.

"People drive an hour to the beach to watch the water. I drive forty-five minutes to look at antiques. That is what I find to be beautiful," she explained. Dad would smile and shrug his shoulders.

I was sure this town is filled with plenty of old stuff. Mom would find it beautiful. I would find it boring. I nudged Mom, and she brought her attention to the waitress.

"French toast and a coffee would be amazing," Mom responded.

"I will have eggs, pancakes, bacon, fruit, and chocolate milk." My stomach gurgled.

"I see someone has worked up her appetite. Good for you, young lady. Are y'all visiting?" asked Nancy. Her hair was basically touching the clouds. It was teased and looked as stiff as the board I had slept on last night. She had a true southern accent, which I loved. I loved just about any accent different from mine. When we had visited different states for vacation, the locals always knew we were from New Jersey. It was crazy how they could pinpoint our exact state. Obviously, I didn't realize we had a strong accent until it was told to us.

"We actually just moved onto the Cooper property."

Nancy pulled her notepad into her chest as she looked surprised.

"Oh, my word, are you related to Pearl Cooper?"

"Yes. She was my great-grandmother." Mom smiled.

"What a blessing. She is well-known around these parts, had the best fruits and vegetables out of the whole town. She was a hardworking woman, that's for sure. It is so great to hear that the property will no longer be vacant. If there is anything you need, don't hesitate to ask. We are all family around these parts."

Gram was right. It already seemed like we were getting a very warm welcome. I wanted to feel it was genuine, but I couldn't be so sure. Nothing else had been to my liking, so we'd see.

"Aw, that is very sweet. I actually need to fix up the place. I need appliances, beds, just about everything."

"Well, you will find it all right here. Everything is within walking distance, and everyone will be happy to help."

"Wonderful. Thank you so much." Mom winked my way, trying to appease me. I still felt doubt swirling around in my head. I couldn't cope with this becoming my permanent residence yet.

"I never heard this kind of country music before. It must be from the 1950s." As I sat waiting for the food, I couldn't help but feel like I was in a time machine, warping me back to the olden days.

"I like it. It goes with the beautiful décor. Makes me feel like I am experiencing the time when Gram grew up," Mom said as she continued staring at all the antiques.

"Yeah, if she grew up in a western movie," I joked.

The food came out, and I could smell the cinnamon from a mile away. Our waitress appeared to be an octopus as she held three trays. She brought one tray just for the syrups. I couldn't believe how many flavors sat in front of me. There were blueberry, maple, strawberry, and salted caramel. I decided to taste test them all as I inhaled my food.

"Wow. Just wow. One positive thing is the food. It melts in my mouth," I said, my mouth full of pancakes.

"It sure does," agreed Mom.

We finished our breakfast and made our way to the hardware store. Walking down each aisle, we filled our cart to the top. I held up a tool I had never seen before.

"What the heck do you do with this?" It looked like a hammer but had a cushion on the end of it. Mom cracked up.

"Well, if we need to hammer a pillow, I think we are set," joked Mom.

"Wow, ma'am, looks like you have a big project on your hands," the cashier said as he looked down at the cart. "And the pillow hammer is a hammer. It just has a protective cushion on the end that you remove," he said with a smile.

Mom and I looked at each other in embarrassment. How did we not realize it was removable?

Mom, already flustered, cleared her throat. "Yes, we sure do. We are fixing up the Cooper property."

"Pearl's place? What a great piece of land." He chuckled. "That is going to be an enormous project over there, though. I have some guys who can help you out." Once again, the generosity of this town continued to surprise me.

"That would be amazing." Mom quickly responded, looking relieved. The cashier continued to ring us up as I wandered over to the window. I, once again, was looking for kids. Unfortunately, not a one in sight.

"Directly across the street, you will find Henry's Furniture. They will be happy to help you. I look forward to seeing what y'all do to the place."

My stomach dropped as I heard Dad's name. I looked at Mom; she looked flustered again. She wasn't the best at hiding her emotions, but she tried. She thanked the cashier as she handed me a few bags. We exited the store and made a pit stop at the car. We loaded the bags in and made our way across the street. I couldn't bring myself to look at the large letters that sat above the store. I just wanted to buy a bed and not be constantly reminded of the absence of Dad. Thankfully, a woman greeted us, not a Henry. She helped us place an order for two beds and a table with chairs.

"What about a couch, Mom?"

"We will just have to use the kitchen chairs for now, sweetie. Trying to keep everything in budget." I couldn't believe this. How was I going to get comfortable on a kitchen chair? Just when I was about to lose it, I saw Mom's attention was on the ground. She tried every possible way to refrain from seeing my disappointment. In that moment, I felt awful. How could I be such a brat? I couldn't have Mom feeling guilty, so I came up with a temporary solution.

"I have a better idea. Pillows on the ground! Talk about comfy."

"I love that idea," Mom replied, smiling.

The morning drew long as we continued on to the appliance store. The man who helped us assured us they would all be delivered by the afternoon. I couldn't believe how accommodating everyone was. We just had one last stop, the grocery store.

We headed into the Piggly Wiggly. I giggled when seeing such a silly name.

"Mom, we still need marshmallows, chocolate, and graham crackers."

"S'mores?" Mom raised her brows, knowing just where my mind was headed.

"You know it!" I skipped down the aisle to grab the items. When I went to grab a bag of marshmallows, I feasted my eyes on a real treat. *Moon Pie? What is this?* I licked my lips as I read the ingredients out loud. "Graham crackers, marshmallow, coated in chocolate." It was a S'mores on the go. I have never seen these in New Jersey. I grabbed an armful and dumped them in the cart. We made our way to the register as I noticed a toddler running down the aisle. Well, I guess there was some life form of children in this town. Too bad they were a quarter of my age.

"Will that be all?" asked the cashier, her name tag reading *Kathleen*.

"Actually, I was wondering if you guys were hiring."

I was shocked to hear Mom ask for a job. She never told me she was interested in working at the grocery store, but I guessed she had no choice.

With no hesitation, the cashier immediately answered, "Absolutely, we could always use a little help. Can you start tomorrow?"

"Tomorrow? You don't need to see my resume or anything?" Mom looked surprised at how fast it was to get a job, considering back in New Jersey, it was close to impossible.

"Oh no, honey, no resume needed. Does ten a.m. work?"

"Ten it is, thank you so much!"

I smiled at Mom, feeling super proud for her. We exited the store, hopped in the car, and headed back to the old, beat-up house.

We bumped up and down as if on a rollercoaster, the dirt road awful for this small rental car.

"I kind of forgot how horrible the house is." I laughed.

"With a little paint and some fixing up, it will be great."

"You mean a lot of paint and a lot of fixing up."

We both laughed and carried the groceries inside. As Mom entered first, she dropped the bag of produce, and apples spilled out onto the dusty floor. She looked as if she had seen a ghost.

I hoped the house wasn't haunted too. I turned to see what she was looking at, when my jaw dropped open. A knotty pine table and chairs were placed to the right of the room. We had just ordered the furniture two short hours earlier. They must have brought it right over. I then saw yellow out of the corner of my eye. I turned to the front door and noticed a note taped on.

"Mom, look." I pointed at the note on the door.

We don't mean to intrude, but we wanted to have this all set up before you returned. You may put the table wherever you'd like. We did place the beds in the room that sits to the left of the upstairs. We agreed that room had the best view. We will be back soon with the appliances. We wish you the best of luck. -The People of Elkville.

My heart fluttered as fast as a hummingbird's wings. These people were genuine after all. Mom shed a tear as she set the groceries on the table.

"Race you to the top!" she yelled. She ran upstairs to feast her eyes on our new bedroom. I ran right behind her. We turned the corner at the top to see both beds, next to one another. A large window faced the side field, where the sun sat.

"Well, it looks like we will have a much better sleep tonight," I said. We returned downstairs to unload the rest of the food. As we waited for the appliances, we decided to try out the old, rusted fire pit.

Stepping over the weeds, we overlooked the property. Mom was jabbering on about all the work she needed to do to the property. I couldn't help but imagine how great our adventures could be out here. It made me instantly miss my friends. They would really love all of this space to play our imaginary games.

As Mom continued to talk while overlooking the land, she tripped right over the firepit. As soon as she laughed at herself, I joined in as well.

"I might not know how to fill a truck with gas, but your father has taught me how to make a pretty great fire." Mom rolled up balls of newspaper and ripped up pieces of our moving boxes. She then stacked thin twigs she collected from the field. There was a large pile of partially rotted firewood off to the side. She grabbed a few pieces and placed them on top. Within minutes, a full-blown fire crackled within the metal pit.

"Go grab the s'mores essentials," Mom instructed. She watched as I took off with excitement in my veins.

Knock, knock.

I made my way to the door. I peeked out the window to see a bunch of men carrying our appliances.

"Mom!" I yelled. She came inside as I motioned her to the door.

"Good evening, ladies. My name is Art. Me and a couple of others wanted to welcome you to town and set up your appliances."

Mom smiled. "Thank you so much. Follow me, I will show you to the kitchen." She walked past me. "Layla, go enjoy that fire. I will be right out."

I sat for about ten minutes, staring into the flames. Mom finally made her way out, handing me a stick.

"Let's make some s'mores."

We toasted the marshmallows and pressed the cracker to the chocolate. The tasty treat squeezed from the side and dripped onto our fingers.

"Dad would have loved this," I said out of the blue.

Mom nodded and smiled. "He sure would have." Swallowing back tears, she tossed her stick into the flames. Mom poured water over the dying flame. It sizzled as smoke lifted into the air. She placed her arm around me as we made our way inside.

"It's getting late. And your mom has work tomorrow. Can you believe it?"

I was happy for Mom, but I felt like I would be lost without her.

"What will I do without you here?"

"You will be just fine. I wrote down the number to the store. I will leave my cellphone here, in case of an emergency. Why don't you use the house as your canvas? You love to paint. You are more than welcome to add some color to these sad walls. Or you can go explore the farm, but don't go too far. I don't want you getting lost in all this land. Let me go tuck you in."

I fell into bed as if I was lying on a cloud. *Ahhhhh.* I let out a large sigh. The new furniture really helped me feel more at home. After snuggling farther under the sheets, Mom kneeled at my bedside.

"Care for a story?"

"Of course." I always loved Mom's stories and imagination. Mom placed her hand over mine.

"There once was a place called the Sky of Bliss. It was a place that sat just above the clouds and was filled with beautiful colors. There were rainbows and clouds that stretched across for miles. The sun beamed down all day without a drop of rain. Butterflies and birds gather there among other wild, exotic creatures." Mom brushed through my hair. "People who travel to this place are granted the most amazing gift, the gift of happiness. A happiness like they have never experienced before. It makes them feel alive. It warms their hearts. It makes everything bad go away."

And just like that, I peacefully dozed off.

****

The sun seemed to be shining extra bright through the windows this morning. Or maybe it was because Mom hadn't gotten around to putting up curtains.

"Are you ready for your first day of work?"

"I sure am. How do I look?"

"Piggly Wiggly fantastic."

Mom laughed.

"Listen, there is plenty of food in the fridge. I don't know how long I will be. So, make sure if you decide to venture out today, stay close to home. Don't talk to strangers. Be safe."

"I will, Mom. Don't worry. I love you."

"I love you too, sweetie."

Mom was right, the walls were sad. I couldn't stand looking at the yellow stains any longer. Good thing all of the colors we picked out were super bright. I figured I would start with our room. I didn't even hesitate on what color to pick. The paint can was almost impossible to open. Pushing a screwdriver under the lip of the lid, I pried it open. Splashing purple paint over the stains came naturally to me. Maybe I would be the next Monet.

An hour of strokes on the wall, and the boredom hit another level. Becoming a famous painter quickly faded from my mind. I decided it was time to explore the field. I ran downstairs and out the back door. My eyes paced back and forth, deciding where to venture first. I headed to my left as I pushed through tall stalks. Some branches pushed back, smacking me in the face. I wondered if any treasures might be buried here. This place had to be super old. If only I had Johnny and Savannah here to help me dig. I would probably need my entire neighborhood to help, considering how big my new yard was. I grabbed a stick and sat down to dig. I couldn't shake the feeling of loneliness. I missed my friends. I missed Dad. My vision became blurred by my tears. I stood up and wiped my eyes. As my vision became clear, I saw something beckoning me in the distance.

"Wow! Cool basket!"

A large woven basket sat in the middle of the field.

"I could fit in this!" I jumped in and pretended to grab the steering wheel. I looked to my right, as Jeff Gordon returned the look. It was on! I jolted side to side, whipping my race car around the track. I imagined I was at the speedway with Dad.

We went once a month to watch the race cars and monster truck show.

As I approached the finish line, a lightbulb went off in my head.

"Could this be another sign from Dad? Maybe the Sky of Bliss is real! I could make my own air balloon with this basket!"

I raced back to the house to grab the sheet off my bed. I also grabbed the battery-operated fan I had in the car, to use as a motor.

"Oh! I have to grab one more thing!"

Back in my room, I had hidden my most prized possession, a picture of Dad. I slid it into the pocket of my black jeans.

"Dad, I am heading into the sky, and you are coming with me!" My arms were filled with supplies as I raced back to the field. First, with wooden clothespins, I hooked the sheet to the basket. I threw in my water bottle and a Moon Pie. I grabbed the fan and leapt inside. My arm extended over my head as I held the fan toward the sheet. The air slowly started to inflate the soft, pink fabric. Before I knew it, it had fully expanded. I was several feet off the ground.

"Whoaaa!!! It's working! Dad, if you are watching, get me to the Sky of Bliss." I looked into the sky, hoping for the best. The basket continued to rise, and I was now even with the clouds. My belly felt as if it had dropped. The small town of Elkville seemed entirely too small now. I couldn't believe I was actually soaring through the sky.

Suddenly, the basket dropped a little. I looked up at the fan and noticed the blades were slowing down.

Whoosh. Just like that, the last blade stopped, and I realized the batteries had died.

What am I going to do? I am too young to die. Why didn't I bring extra batteries?

My worries continued growing. I became much too distracted to pay attention to my surroundings. When a sudden gust of wind whipped me around the sky, I gave a scream of surprise. I realized two things at once. First, I could no longer control the basket. Second, I was beyond afraid and had no Plan B.

"Dad, I need help," I mumbled under my breath.

I closed my eyes and held on tight. My knuckles whitened as I held on for dear life. The turbulence continued until I slammed down. My eyes slowly opened to see a very dark and ominous place. A small amount of light peeked through the clouds. It was just enough light to see what surrounded me. It appeared to be storm clouds, completely enclosed around me. I could no longer see below or above. A thick fog swarmed me. A chill went down my back. The silence was almost scary.

Where am I? I am probably so far from the Sky of Bliss. How will I ever get back down? I hesitantly put one foot in front of the other as I walked along the length of the basket.

"What is that? Is it coming towards me?" My hands clammed up, and the sweat formed on my brow. A dark figure seemed to be making its way toward me.

"Hello? Who is that?"

"Hey, over there!"

.

CHAPTER 5
Cautious

Who could this be?

The figure got closer and closer.

My hair became stuck to my forehead. A whirlpool spun in my stomach. Was I in danger?

"Well, hello. My name is Roy. Who are you?" The boy stood just a little taller than I did. He was dressed in all black; his hair was dark as well as his eyes. His black Converse sneakers were untied, and he seemed to be disoriented.

"Hi, Roy. My name is Layla. Where am I?"

Roy looked around. "Your guess is as good as mine. I am up here in search of my colors. I seemed to have lost them. I don't normally appear this dark."

I could totally relate. I was always known for wearing the brightest colors, but since Dad passed, my wardrobe matched my feelings. A flash of that purple paint popped into my head. If only I could come back to life, like the walls.

"Well, I am in search of the Sky of Bliss. Have you ever heard of it?"

"Hmmm... sounds familiar." He shrugged. "Maybe we can help each other. Maybe this Sky of Bliss place has my missing colors! Can I join you?"

I so desperately wanted a friend, considering this new town seemed to have no other kids my age. I also figured the company would help me feel less nervous.

"Of course. I just hope we can make it through this place. I can barely see a thing."

Roy nodded his head in agreement.

"So why do you need to get to the Sky of Bliss?"

"Well, my mom said it is the most beautiful place. It brings happiness to all who visit."

"Are you not happy?"

"Lately, I haven't been."

Roy's face looked broken for me. "Well, I hope we find this place and it can help you."

Nerves continued as I tripped over my water bottle. It must have fallen out of the basket when I crashed.

"Thank you. So where are you from?" I wanted to know how he was able to get up in the sky. I also hoped he lived close by. I could really use a friend who was up for adventure.

"The sky, of course!"

I was shocked. How was that even possible?

"Wow, I didn't know people could live up here."

"Well, I'm not your average person." He shrugged.

"Are you some kind of alien?"

Roy laughed. "No, but that would be pretty cool. When I find my colors, I will be back to my bright self; you'll see."

Roy and I pushed our way through the fog. Things kept continuing to get darker and darker. The silence lingered on.

"Roy, are you still there? I can barely see."

"Yup, still here. I do..." He stopped. "Wait. What is that up ahead? It looks like there may be someone else here."

Another dark figure appeared ahead of us.

"Hey! Who is that up there?" yelled Roy.

There was no response.

"Is this safe? The closer we get, the darker it is getting..." I anxiously wiped my sweaty hands on my pants.

"I am starting to think this is the wrong way," Roy whispered to me. "Who is up there? Answer us!"

"Well, hello, Roy," a super deep voice called out. "Hello, Layla."

The voice instantly created goosebumps on both of our arms.

"Do I know you?" Roy asked.

"You will soon." There was a low chuckle. "I am here to take the color from this world. The name is Darkness, Mr. Darkness."

Roy and I stopped dead in our tracks.

"Layla, I think it is time to turn around."

"But what if the Sky of Bliss is this way? I can't give up!" I wasn't going to let anything stand in my way of happiness. A flood of memories poured in my head. Dad was taking his turn in charades. Mom and I were rolling around in laughter. I needed those feelings back. I had to push on.

"Well, what do you suggest we do?"

"Let's see if we can negotiate," I whispered.

The closer we got, the clearer the figure became. Mr. Darkness appeared to be very tall in stature—scary tall. The vibes he was giving off felt negative and cold. It reminded me of the time I played hide and seek over at my neighbor's house. His basement was cold and spooky. I hid under the steps for an entire hour. I was freezing and afraid. The only reason I sat there for so long, was because I was super competitive and didn't want to be found. After constant chills and fear, I escaped my hiding spot and went back upstairs. My neighbor, Timmy, told me he never went downstairs because it was haunted. The chills ran through my body and I never went back to his house. Mr. Darkness was giving me those same chills.

"That's it. Come a little closer," Mr. Darkness crooned.

Roy gulped.

I was trying hard to overcome my fear.

"What is it that you want from us?"

"Your color, of course," Mr. Darkness responded, letting out a creepy chuckle.

"Tough luck. I lost my colors. Looks like you can let us pass through now," Roy called out.

The creepy laugh came again.

"Nice try. Pay the price, or no entrance."

"Is it me, or is his voice getting deeper and deeper?" Roy gulped.

I looked down, only to realize I was dressed completely in black. My shirt was all black as well as my pants. Even my sneakers were black. What could I offer? I reached my hand into my pockets to see if I had a coin or anything to offer.

And there was my picture. I stared down at Dad. My eyes started to swell as tears piled up. His smile flashed in my head as it brought back all the amazing memories we had shared. I couldn't give this away to such a horrible creature. I couldn't lose this too.

"I can't push through this journey without you, Dad." Yet I knew I would never find my happiness if I didn't hand it over.

"Roy, I have something with color. I will give it to Mr. Darkness so we can continue on," I interrupted, close to letting those tears drift down my cheeks.

"Why don't you sound excited about it?"

"It is a picture of my dad. He passed away several months ago." I stared at the picture, a few tears escaping.

"Oh," Roy whispered. "Oh, I am so sorry, Layla. You cannot give this up. Maybe we can trick him."

"We can barely see as it is. There is no other option."

"Give me your colors now!" demanded Mr. Darkness. The voice echoed for miles as the goosebumps remained on our arms.

"Are you sure you have nothing else with color?" Roy asked under his breath.

"I'm sure." I stepped closer to the darkness. I slowly held out my hand. My fingers curled protectively around the picture.

"Stop," yelled Roy suddenly. "Your hair!"

"What?" I slowly took a step back, away from the darkness. "What about it?"

"Wasn't your hair pulled back when I first saw you?"

"Yes. It still is," I said in confusion. *What is he getting at?*

"What color is your scrunchie?"

I gasped. "Oh!" I totally forgot I had the most colorful scrunchie in my hair! I whipped it out and threw it in the direction of Mr. Darkness as he walked toward me.

He stopped and stared in amazement at all the colors as he slowly worked his magic to make them disappear.

"Let's go!" yelled Roy.

Roy and I ran past Mr. Darkness. Things immediately started to lighten up.

"Thank you for helping me back there." I tucked the picture back into my pocket, keeping it safe once again.

"No, you helped me. I can't believe you were willing to give up your picture."

I smiled. I was excited that we were one step closer to happiness. I also felt grateful to have made a new friend.

Walking through the fog, we kept pretty quiet. About thirty minutes had passed, but there was still nothing in sight.

"So how is it down on Earth?" asked Roy.

"Hardly exciting." I shrugged. A few months ago, my response would have been much different. I was stuck in sadness, and this new town only made me feel worse.

"Earth looks amazing from my view."

"My life on Earth used to be amazing. After my dad died, things became pretty awful. I had to move away from all of my friends. My mom and I are now living in a broken-down house, basically in the middle of nowhere."

"That does sound pretty awful. But what about the colors?" asked Roy.

"What colors?" I was unsure of what Roy meant.

"Doesn't Earth have the most bright and beautiful colors?"

What is his thing with color? I shrugged.

"Well, yes, there is a variety of colors."

"Bright colors can create happiness. When I had my colors, I always made people smile."

"I will keep that in mind."

We skipped along, until my skip started to turn into a slow walk.

"Oh no. What are we in for now?" I asked in fear.

Roy looked up, only to see another dark figure approaching.

"Just great. If this is another color-snatching thief, I am out of here."

I grabbed his hand. "Roy, it will be fine; let's go." He sighed as I called out, "Hey, who is that up there?"

A boy's voice answered, "Ray here! And who may you guys be?"

"Ray? Is that really you?" Roy called out.

"Roy?!" he gasped. "What are you doing in my parts of the sky?"

I turned towards Roy.

"You know this Ray?"

"Yes. But he lives on the opposite side of the sky as I do." Roy couldn't understand how Ray was able to get all the way over here. He blamed the fog and Mr. Darkness.

"I am looking for my colors, and my friend Layla, here, she is looking for the Sky of Bliss. Any chance you may know where that is?"

"Not too sure. I, too, am looking for something, though." Ray's shoulders drooped. "I seemed to have lost my warmth."

"Well, maybe we can find it at the Sky Of Bliss. Why don't you join us?" I suggested.

"That would be great!" Ray walked closer to Roy and me. He also seemed to be the same age as I am. He had a bright yellow shirt on with ripped jeans. His hair matched perfectly to his shirt.

"We could have used you a moment ago," I mumbled under my breath. I wished he had come along earlier so the negotiation had gone a little smoother.

"What was that?" Ray asked.

"Oh, nothing; let's keep going."

The three of us walked side by side as we ventured on to find the Sky Of Bliss.

CHAPTER 6
Intense

"So how did you both end up in this scary world after all?" I questioned the two. Even though Roy and Ray lived in the sky, they seemed to be just as lost as I was.

"My part of the sky is filled with brightness and beauty." Roy smiled as he appeared to daydream. "All of a sudden, my colors seemed to disappear." His smile quickly turned to a frown. "I searched and searched and decided to travel far across the sky to find them. It seems I ended up here." Roy shivered. "It got dark so quickly, and then the fog came. Not only did I lose my colors, but I seemed to have lost my way."

Ray nodded. "My warmth is very important to me. I can't survive long if I am not warm. When it started to fade, I became desperate. I searched and searched and have traveled far and wide across this sky. I, too, seem to have lost my way." Ray frowned.

"Well then, I guess we all have something in common," I said.

"So, what exactly is this Sky Of Bliss?" Ray shivered as his lips tinted blue. He had never heard of it and was curious to see if his warmth might be there.

"My mom says it is the most beautiful place in the sky, and there is a feeling of happiness when you reach it. It sounded like the most amazing, welcoming, warm and fuzzy type of place," I whispered. "She tells me the best bedtime stories that seem so real. I had to try to find this place."

Ray shook his shoulders as he let out a breath that became visible.

"Speaking of warm, does it feel like it is getting colder?" Roy shivered.

"Now that you mention it, I do feel a chill in the air." I began feeling very nervous for Ray as I glanced over in his direction.

"The temperature does seem to be dropping."

The three of us continued on, trying our hardest to warm up. Ray rubbed his hands together. I jumped up and down to get my blood flowing. The air grew as crisp as a snowy winter storm.

"I think we are headed for a cold front." Roy's fingertips were starting to freeze together.

"I don't think we should continue. I won't be able to withstand the c-c-cold," Ray stammered.

"I have come so far. I need to push forward to find my happiness. What can we do to create warmth?"

"Should we stand close to one another? Body heat can help," suggested Roy.

"Good idea," I said.

We immediately huddled around each another, trying to create a more comfortable atmosphere for Ray.

"I don't think this is working. I am starting to feel w-weak." Ray's eyelids fluttered as they were almost completely closed.

"Imagination!" I yelled, causing Ray to jump in surprise.

"Huh?"

Ray and Roy looked at one another and Roy shrugged.

"Down on Earth, we have snowstorms. They can sometimes be unbearable. So sometimes in the winter, my mom would tell me to close my eyes and think of something warm and use my imagination to feel better. I would always think of a sunny beach. I would picture the sun beating down and the sweat dripping down my face. It would actually help me heat up," I explained.

"I have nothing to lose," said Ray.

I squealed. Jumping up and down, I couldn't wait to introduce my imaginary adventures with my new friends.

"Okay. I want us all to close our eyes. Picture us in the hottest place..."

"Uh-h w-where?" Ray stuttered.

"Let's travel to Ecuador. I learned in school that Ecuador is named after the equator. It also has lovely mountains and jungles to explore. Let's visit one of those jungles." I peeked my eyes open to see them both nodding. "Okay, imagine the sun is beaming directly down on us." I waited a minute before asking, "Are you guys warming up yet?"

"I am starting to." Roy swung his body around, accidentally stumbling into Ray.

"A little bit; let's keep exploring Ecuador. This is one of my favorite places," Ray said.

We ran across the sky as if we were running wild in the jungle. We leaped in laughter. The tall green trees stretched far and wide. We could now hear the tropical birds calling out.

"Oh, wow! Look at that monkey! He seems to want us to follow him." I giggled.

"Hey, wait for us, monkey!" yelled Roy.

"He is so fast!" yelled Ray.

We all burst into laughter as we followed the friendly monkey. His thin tail wrapped around the branches of the tall trees. He seemed to have brought us to a glistening waterfall. He motioned with his hands to enter the cascading water.

"Wow! This looks just like the waterfall my mom used to take me to when we played imaginary games. It can transport you to just about anywhere in the world."

"Are you warming up, Ray?" asked Roy as he looked to the sun peeking through the treetops.

"Almost. Let's have this waterfall transport us to the hottest desert," responded Ray.

I cleared my throat, getting ready to recite the words to teleport us. As much as I wanted to transport us to the Sky Of Bliss, I needed guaranteed warmth for Ray. My dad always told me to think of others before myself. I knew what I needed to do.

"Magical waterfall, do your trick. Send us to the hottest desert, lickety-split."

The waterfall whipped us up into the air. We twirled around like a tornado. Disappearing from the jungle, we popped into a new location. And just like that, we had landed on the dry and fiery hot desert. A sign sat before us that read, *Welcome To Death Valley, California.*

I instantly felt on fire. I looked over at Roy, as he wiped the sweat that immediately formed on his head.

"No wonder this place is called Death Valley. It is so hot, my death seems to be approaching," joked Roy.

"I feel right at home." Ray laughed.

"I am glad this place is warming you up, but I could use water right about now." I sat down, feeling exhausted. Sweat dripped down my back as I looked over to Ray. "Well? Are you feeling—"

"Did you just hear that?" Roy interrupted.

"Hear what?" asked Ray.

Sssssssssssss.

"I think I just heard a snake."

"Quit being a baby. We are fine." Ray smirked.

"Shut it, Ray." Roy pushed Ray's shoulder.

"I need more heat!"

"Guys, enough! Listen!" I yelled as the boys immediately got quiet.

Sssssssssssssssssssssss.

"Oh no! Rattlesnake!" I jumped quickly to my feet. "A book I once read told me all about snakes in deserts. This one appears to be a Sidewinder Rattlesnake. They are extremely poisonous!" I anxiously backed up. "What should we do?"

Roy cried, "Run!"

We all took off, dirt flying behind us. Winded and hot, we came to a slow down.

"Ray, are you good now?" I asked, panting.

"After this heat and all that running, I should be warmed up for days," Ray muttered as he tried catching his breath.

I was so ready to get out of there. "Okay, Roy and Ray, time to come out of our imagination, in five, four, three, two, one!"

We all opened our eyes to find that the heavy fog from before surrounded us.

"I never thought I'd say this, but I am glad to be back here," said Roy.

We all laughed as the anxiety wore off and we could all breathe properly again.

"Thank you for the adventure, Layla. I don't think I have ever been more afraid and excited at the same time," Ray commented.

"As long as you have warmed up, I am happy to help."

After an hour of adventure, we had overcome another obstacle standing in my way of finding happiness. Onward and upward, we walked on, to find the Sky Of Bliss.

****

Two hours later...

Exhaustion started to set in. We were all desperate to reach the place that could potentially help us all.

"I am starting to get sleepy from all this walking, any chance we can take a little break?" asked Roy.

"I could use a little rest," answered Ray.

"Yes, I agree, and I'm starving! What do you do for food up here?" I curiously asked.

Roy and Ray looked at each other and smiled.

"Do you like marshmallows?" Ray asked.

"They are my favorite!"

They reached down toward the cloud as Ray said, "Remember that imagination you often use?"

"Mmhmmm."

"Well. picture this piece of cloud is a marshmallow." He smiled at my excited squeal.

I closed my eyes and placed the cloud into my mouth. I slowly chewed it before declaring, "That was the best marshmallow I ever had and I have had my fair share of marshmallows!"

"I think I need some of that," said Roy.

The three of us sat in a circle as we pinched off pieces of cloud and devoured them.

"You guys are the best." I smiled at Roy and Ray.

This scary place didn't seem so scary anymore. Not because it wasn't, but because I finally didn't feel so alone. I was reminded of Savannah and Johnny and our adventures together. I was happy to have friends to share in fun moments again.

"Who wants to—" Ray stopped speaking as we saw a dark figure headed our way. "Guys, seems we may have some company," he warned, pointing.

"And just when I thought things were getting less complicated," Roy moaned.

I looked ahead, squinting. "Hello up there," I called out.

"Who is that?" the figure called back. The voice seemed soft and gentle.

"Layla."

"And Roy."

"And Ray."

The figure seemed to slowly go back the other way.

"Can we help you?" I asked. I felt relaxed in this moment. I couldn't quite figure out why. I just knew this person was not here to cause us harm.

"I don't want any trouble. I am just looking for my friends."

"We won't give you any trouble. We are in search of things, too. You can join us," I gently offered.

"That would be awfully nice of you." The figure paused. "Are you sure?" It started to inch back over.

"Of course! The more, the merrier. What is your name?"

"My name is Liss."

A girl appeared before us. She looked to be a year or two younger than I was. She wore a white, puffy jacket. Her hair was platinum blonde with wavy ends. She appeared to be afraid.

"Hi, Liss, I am Roy. I am searching for my colors."

"I am Ray. I am searching for my warmth."

"I am Layla." I stood tall. "And I am looking for the Sky Of Bliss. Any chance you have heard of it?"

"Sorry to say, I don't believe so."

"Well, maybe your friends are there. Or maybe we will run into them along the way," I optimistically reassured her.

Liss timidly looked down. She nodded her head in agreement, although she still seemed to be guarded.

CHAPTER 7
Determined

So what do your friends look like?" Roy asked Liss.

"Well, they look a lot like me, but that doesn't help much when we are here. It is so dark in this place... I miss them so much. We did everything together."

Roy rolled his eyes. "You can blame that on Mr. Darkness." He placed his hand on Liss's shoulder. "We will find them for you."

Liss's shyness started to ease as she lifted her head and smiled at Roy. "We usually travel the sky together, but somehow we ended up here. With all the darkness, we couldn't see a thing.

One by one, they all disappeared. I have been looking for them ever since."

I cleared my throat as I broadened my shoulders. "My gut tells me we will find the colors, warmth, and your friends at the Sky Of Bliss."

Liss shrugged her shoulders. I didn't get to tell her about our destination. "What is—"

"The Sky Of Bliss holds the brightest colors," Roy jumped to explain. "It creates the most welcoming feelings. You will be left with pure happiness. A happiness unlike anything else. Birds and butterflies fly around. I am sure your friends might be there, as well as my colors, and Ray's warmth. Layla is taking us all there!" Roy's excitement became contagious.

"Wow! Have you ever been there, Layla?" asked Liss.

"Unfortunately not. Even though my life before seemed pretty close to it." I pouted as I remembered life before. I had it all, a happy family, a loving mom and dad, wonderful friends, and super fun Saturday nights. The more I thought about it, the more tears formed in my eyes. I tried my hardest to not let them see. I wiped my eyes, not giving my tears any chance of falling.

Boooooom.

"Did you hear that?" asked Ray. *Crassshhhhh.*

"Did you see that?" asked Roy.

The clouds beneath our feet started to shake. Losing our balance, we began stumbling around.

"Oh no," Liss cried. "This is not good. It seems like we may be walking right into a thunderstorm."

Thunder continued to bang. Lightning flashed before our eyes. The rain trickled down our faces.

I couldn't help but think I was the one to blame. I insisted on going this way. I insisted on finding the Sky Of Bliss, despite all the obstacles we had already faced. "I am sorry, guys. I have pushed us so far, and things keep getting worse. The Sky Of Bliss probably doesn't even exist." Thankfully, the rain masked my tears. I couldn't stop thinking of Dad. He always protected me in difficult times. I also thought of Mom. If something happened to me, it would ruin her. I never should have left the house.

"Layla, we would have never escaped Mr. Darkness if it wasn't for you."

"And we would have never overcome the cold if it wasn't for you." Ray smiled.

"And we will overcome this too! Because we have you!" Liss cheered. It was the first time Liss was smiling big.

The wind swirled around us like a tornado. The rain poured down. I could barely see. We all huddled together, trying to protect one another.

"I don't want anything bad to happen to us," I whispered. "The rain and winds are getting stronger." I wanted to be brave, but it appeared we were in the middle of a hurricane.

"We can do this!" Ray shouted.

The wind and rain got worse.

I sniffled as I looked to my friends. "We can do this," I said with some uncertainty. I wanted to be brave. "We can do this," I repeated, remembering how far we had already come. I couldn't give up now.

Whoooooooosh. The wind stirred faster and faster.

"Guys! The wind is pulling me!" I cried out.

"Oh no!" Roy cried.

The wind pulled me up and off my feet. "Help!"

"How will we get her down?" Roy shouted in worry.

"Layla, try to reach for my hand," Ray called out. His voice was soft against the pounding rain.

My body tumbled around as I tried to reach for Ray. I front flipped then fell towards the sky. It was as if the wind was playing a game with me, one that I clearly was losing.

"Ray?"

The rain poured down so heavily that I had a hard time seeing his hand. Every time I grabbed him, my fingers were tugged. "I don't think I can—" Thunder rumbled, blocking out my words. I shivered. In that moment, Dad popped into my head. He was giving me a thumbs up. He did this every time I was scared to try something new or do something that scared me. I couldn't let him down.

"Wait! Remember when we pulled up the clouds to eat?"

"Layla, how can you be hungry at a time like this!" Roy shouted.

A vision of *It's A Wonderful Life* flashed before my eyes. In the movie, George told Mary he would lasso the moon for her. Maybe this would work for me.

"No, I don't mean food. We need to use the clouds! We need to shape them into a lasso."

"Okay, and then what?" Ray held his arm over his eyes, as he tried to shield the rain and focus in on my direction.

"I need one of you to try your hardest to throw the lasso around me. Then you must all pull me down."

Liss dropped to her knees. "I will make the lasso!" She grabbed a chunk of cloud and started molding it into a perfect rope. Her hands became a blur to my eyes. I tried my hardest to stay close to my friends.

"Okay, I have it," said Liss.

"I will lasso Layla," Roy called out. He grabbed the rope and started to swing it into a circular motion. "Ready!"

Roy threw the lasso into the sky, but the wind whipped it past me. Without giving up, he once again threw the lasso up. This time, it was a perfect throw. The rope secured itself around me.

"You've got me! Pull me down!" My lips quivered as nerves took over.

Roy, Ray, and Liss pulled as if they were competing in a tug of war, and I inched closer and closer.

"Got you!" Liss said. With a final tug, they had me back on the ground. My friends quickly surrounded me, embracing me, as I continued to shake.

"Thank you so much," I told them. "Now let's keep moving. I think we are close to passing this storm." I couldn't believe how they'd saved me. I felt very grateful to have them.

Roy, Ray, Liss, and I held hands as we pushed through the wind and rain. Slowly, the rain started to lighten up, but the wind seemed to follow, nipping at our legs and arms. The minutes began feeling like hours. We were all becoming exhausted. Ray yawned. Roy stretched his arms out. Liss wiped her eyes. My legs began feeling like heavy weights.

"Now that we have passed the storm, why don't we have a camp out, so we can get some rest?" I immediately envisioned my backyard sleepovers. Dad would set up a tent for me and Savannah. We would spend the night making crafts, using nature. The night would always end with us looking up at the stars and falling fast asleep.

"Camp out? What is that?" asked Roy.

"Camping was always my Dad and my favorite thing to do together. He would even set up a tent in my backyard for me and my friends. The best part was when we sat by the bonfire. It was always so bright and warm and the best for making s'mores!" I said in excitement.

"The bright colors must be magnificent" Roy said. I imagined he was missing his colors in that moment.

"The warmth sounds delightful," Ray commented.

"What are s'mores?" asked Liss, to which the others nodded, looking confused.

I couldn't believe they had never heard of s'mores. "The yummiest dessert you will ever have! You make a sandwich out of graham crackers, chocolate, and the fluffiest marshmallow... and then eat it, of course!" I licked my lips.

"The fluffy marshmallow sounds fantastic," Liss says.

"Layla, can you take us camping through your imagination?" asked Ray.

"Yes! Just like we went to the desert for Ray," Roy added.

"Absolutely! First, we must set up the tent." I started to lay out the pieces of the tent, showing Roy, Ray, and Liss how to fit them all together. "We now pitch the tent into the ground, so it doesn't fall apart."

Hammering away, the tent kept flopping around every time one of us got a stake in the ground.

"Oh, come on!" Ray threw his arms down in frustration. I could tell everyone was feeling just as annoyed as I was.

"This wind needs to leave," I muttered.

"Well, at least it stopped storming otherwise," Liss said.

"Let's each try grabbing a side," Roy suggested.

I was over the wind. It seemed to be ruining all of my great moments. We each held a side down, and finally, the tent was secured.

"Perfect! Great job, guys. Now let's get this bonfire going."

We each grabbed a handful of wood, and soon, I got the fire going. I thought of Mom and how proud she would be of this fire. Dad had taught Mom, and I had learned from her.

"We are missing something," I stated. "Oh! Liss, can you grab that fluffy cloud for our marshmallows?"

"I sure can!" Liss grabbed small fluffs of cloud and handed them over.

I showed my friends how to toast the marshmallows over the fire. "This is—" *Whooooosh*. Just as we were toasting, and I started to get the other s'mores supplies, a big wind blew out the fire. "Oh, come on! Leave us alone already!" I yelled. I threw my arms up in frustration. "You brought me to this horrible place! You lifted me into the thunderstorm! You tried blowing my tent away! And now you are ruining our s'mores!"

"I'm really not all that bad," a voice called out.

"Who is that?" I looked side to side. "Did you hear—" Roy, Ray, and Liss all nodded before I could finish my question.

Whooooooooosh. The wind whipped through my hair as I frowned. "The name is Gus."

CHAPTER 8
Fearful

A re you looking to take my color?" asked Roy.

"Or my warmth?" Ray demanded, anxiously pacing back and forth.

"Did you by chance see my friends?" asked Liss.

Gus giggled. "I am not here to take anything," he said.

I mumbled under my breath, "You might not be here to take anything, but you sure do ruin a lot." I couldn't help but feel like Gus was to blame for all the mishaps.

"My job up here in the sky is guidance," Gus retorted as he whipped around me.

It gave me a tickle, as I giggled. "Well, then can you guide us to the Sky Of Bliss?"

"Funny you ask that," said Gus. "Watch."

A bright light burst near us. We all quickly covered our eyes to not be blinded.

"What is that?" asked Roy.

"I don't know, but whatever it is, it is brighter than I am! I never experienced anything brighter than me!" Ray said, sounding surprised.

"Do you think my friends are close by?"

"Gus, think you could guide us away from this?" I asked.

Silence.

"Gus? Are you there?" I put my hand over my eyes to shield the light.

Gus was no longer responding.

"What do you think happened to Gus?" Roy's voice cracked. "Do you think the light got him?"

"I am not sure, but I think we need to all push forward and try to get away from this light." I started to feel defeated once again but knew I needed to stay positive for my friends.

"You're right. Let's go." Ray's quick pace turned into a fast forward walk as we all joined him. But the faster we walked, the brighter the light became, surrounding us completely.

"If this light doesn't go away soon, we need to figure out how to block it," I insisted.

"I have no ideas. Blocking light is not my forte'," Ray shrugged.

"I don't have experience blocking light, either," said Roy.

"Liss, do you have any ideas?" I asked.

Silence once again filled the air.

"Liss?"

Once again, I got no response.

"Oh no! Liss must have gone the other direction. This isn't good. Liss! Liss! Can you hear us?" I yelled.

Still, there was no response.

"How do we even know if *we* are going the right way anymore?" Roy complained.

"I have an idea. Down on Earth, when a cloud covers the sun, it creates shade."

"How dare them." Ray placed his hands on his hips. "I will need to talk to these clouds and—"

"No, Ray, shade can be nice sometimes. It allows us to cool off. But most importantly, it helps if it is *too* bright out."

"It is never too bright for me! Well, minus right now," Ray admitted.

"So, what do you suggest we do?" Roy asked me.

"We must feel around for the clouds. Then we will form them over our head to block out the bright light."

"Great idea, Layla!" Roy smiled.

"I am still against this idea, but I guess we have no other option," Ray protested but threw his arms to his sides.

The three of us started collecting pieces of cloud. When our arms felt full, we began pushing our pieces together.

"How are you guys making out?" I asked, needing to close my eyes again.

"I am just about done."

I opened my eyes, squinting. Roy's clouds were misshaped, but he had created a large barrier.

"Me too." Ray had a smoother shape, but he hadn't grabbed as many pieces.

"Okay, we need to push them all together. We will use our voices to move closer to one another. I will call your name, and you will walk toward my voice. Roy, follow my voice."

"Okay!" Roy called out.

"Got it," Ray said.

"Roy, follow my voice."

Roy carried his large cloud masterpiece toward me. His eyes were shut tightly and he staggered with each step he took.

"Great, Roy! You are right near me. Let's push our clouds together."

Both Roy and I pushed the clouds together to make one large arch. We depended on touch, considering our eyes remained squinted.

"This is big, but we need you, Ray," said Roy.

"Ray, follow my voice," I called out.

When Ray didn't come under our arch, I tried calling again.

"Ray? Are you close?"

"Ray?" Roy called out.

Still silence.

"Oh no! What is going on?"

"First Gus, then Liss, and now Ray! We need to hurry and block this light out!" I dropped to my knees, scooping piles of clouds in my arms. I handed piece by piece to Roy as he molded them together.

"Layla, I think we have enough. You grab one side, and I'll grab the other. Then we will hold it over our heads."

The two of us grabbed onto each side and threw it above us. The light beamed, but the cloud seemed to be working.

"Roy, it is blocking it! We just need to keep pushing forward. This light has to pass at some point."

The possible end to our journey felt bittersweet. I was afraid Roy and I might disappear like the rest of them, but I also felt hopeful. Maybe this bright light meant we were getting close to the Sky of Bliss. Mom did say it was bright and beautiful. I started to think that maybe we could be in the Sky of Bliss. "I feel like the Sky of Bliss is so close," I told Roy.

"I sure hope so," he replied.

"I think it will be filled with all of your colors. I think it will be magical. Maybe we will meet creatures, never known to mankind. What do you think?" My mind raced as all the possibilities flooded in.

"If this place creates happiness, I definitely feel my colors will be there. Think we will find our friends there too?"

"I hope so! But for the first time in a long time, I have a good feeling we will find them. I feel very lucky to have met you all. You became my first friend up here." Although I couldn't see Roy's reaction, I knew he was smiling with me. "What will you do when you find your colors?"

No response.

"Roy?"

And just like that, I was now alone. Fear set in. I started running. I didn't care which way I was going at this point. I didn't want to disappear next. I needed to get my happiness! I needed to return home! My hair whipped behind me. My arms swung back and forth. I ran. And ran. The bright light continued to follow. My breathing picked up. I felt like I was going nowhere. I then stopped dead in my tracks when a figure appeared before me. My face grew pale.

"Hey, squirt!"

Was I dreaming?

"Dad?"

CHAPTER 9
Happiness

Numbness overcame my body. My eyes swelled and the tears began streaming down my cheeks.

Dad slowly walked towards me. "Hi, my sweet girl."

"D-Dad."

He bent down and extended his arms.

"Dad!" I ran forward and threw myself into his arms. And just like that, all of my worries melted away. He was my safe haven. "I have missed you so much." My voice trembled as I tried to compose myself, my face buried in his shoulder.

Dad wiped my tears as he kissed my forehead. "I have missed you enormously," he said, smiling.

My tears finally let up and I pulled back to stare at Dad. I looked at the blond waves in his hair. I studied his hazel eyes; they had always captured my attention. The greenish-gray hues twinkled. I wanted to photograph his face, for I knew this moment would not last forever, even though I prayed it would. "What are you doing here? Am I in Heaven?"

"No, my sweet girl. I knew you needed me and came as quickly as I could." His hand rubbed over my messy brown hair.

He was always there when I needed him the most. I thought about all the times I'd struggled in school, gotten hurt, or was let down by my friends. But this time was different. This time, he wasn't really there and the pain I felt inside was unbearable.

"I was very impressed by your homemade balloon," Dad said then, giving me a smirk.

"You know about the balloon?" My mind raced. "How? You weren't there!"

"Well, how do you think you were pulled up here?"

The awful Gus pulled me here. I sighed. "Uh, the wind?"

"Exactly."

"So, are you able to watch me?"

"Yes, yes, I am. But in that moment, I was actually the one who pulled you here."

I gaped. "Wait... Are you Gus?" I felt silly asking that question. I felt like I was losing it.

"Guilty." Dad chuckled at my gasp.

"Why did you bring me to such a stranded and dark place? I needed to get to the Sky of Bliss." I pulled away from Dad as I crossed my arms. *Doesn't he understand how lonely and sad I am without him?*

"This might be hard to believe, but you are in the Sky of Bliss, Layla."

I snorted. "How? Mom said it was beautiful! She said it was bright and colorful and was filled with butterflies and pure happiness."

Dad put his arm around my shoulder and pulled me in close. "The Sky of Bliss only appears to the eye of what the heart is feeling. It can't bring you happiness. You must find happiness within yourself, in order to view the beauty of this place."

I still didn't quite understand. "Who were all the people I met along the way?"

"They were lessons." I couldn't imagine what valuable lesson I was supposed to take away from defeating a color snatcher. I didn't know how fighting the cold or surviving a thunderstorm could help me find happiness, either. "Exactly what lessons was I supposed to learn?"

"Well, Roy represents the rainbow. Roy needed to find his color. But, really, he wanted you to get color back into your life. You need to view the world like you did when I was still with you. See the beauty in everything."

Things were starting to make sense. My eyes teared up once again.

"Ray represented the sun. He needed to find his warmth, just like you do. You need to have moments of warmth and comfort. I can't be there to wrap my arms around you and create it, but I will always be watching over you. You need to remember to see the bright side of situations and create your own comfort."

Dad was right. I needed to be confident and secure on my own.

"Liss represents the cumulus clouds. She needed to find her friends. Cumulus clouds are beautiful on their own, but they also exude beauty when coming together with other clouds. You will always be beautiful, but you need to let others in. Just because you left everything you know, doesn't mean you won't create new memories with new faces. Friends are important. They will help you in the hard times. Branch out and be open to making friends in your new town."

"Dad, I—"

He pulled me back into his arms. "I know our situation doesn't seem fair. I agree, but life must go on. I can only be fully happy if I see my little girl happy again. Embrace this new life. I promise you, I will be here every step of the way. Any time you feel the breeze, know, in that moment, I am standing by your side."

Overcome, I squinted my eyes shut as several tears dropped to the clouds under my feet. As I slowly opened my eyes, I gasped. The bluest sky stretched for miles, a rainbow appearing before me with the most beautiful colors I had ever seen. The sun was shining brighter than ever, its warmth kissing my cheeks. The beams stretched far and wide. Looking down, I saw cumulus clouds gathering under and floating up to rest around me. They were so fluffy and filled me with such joy. "Wow."

Butterflies of every color fluttered around me and Dad. I let out a giggle as they tickled my nose with their wings. Birds of all shapes and sizes flew in unison behind the butterflies. They all slowly came together and made a perfect heart in the sky. "Wow! Now this is the Sky of Bliss," I whispered, clinging to Dad.

"My girl has found her happiness!" Dad grinned, sending me a wink. His smile faded a moment later. "As much as I want this to last forever, your mom would kill me if I didn't return you home."

"Oh, yeah." I knew Mom needed me. She was staying so strong through all of this, but she was hurting just as much as I was. "Dad, I wish you could come home with me. You would love the farm! It has—"

"My favorite part of the farm is the fire pit," he interrupted. "And that field is unreal! With your adventurous side and your mom's imagination, you guys could really create something great there."

I knew in that moment that Dad was really looking over us. I couldn't wait to tell Mom. I hope this brought her comfort. "Dad, I am going to miss you so much!" I held on to him just a little bit longer.

Roy, Ray, and Liss appeared next to Dad, holding my homemade air balloon. Dad held my hand to help me climb in. I looked back at them one last time as they waved, smiling.

"I will carry you back home safely," Dad promised. "Now remember, if you ever feel a wind, it's just Dad checking up on you. When you need guidance, I will be there." He smiled. "I love you forever and always."

I wiped the tears that continued to flow. I blew him a kiss and he caught it with his hand before he vanished. The air balloon lifted off the clouds and was carried through the sky. I looked over the fields and houses as I made my way back home. When I reached the farm, I was slowly lowered down to the field.

I hopped out. "Thanks, Dad. I love you!" With the breeze at my back, nudging me forward, I raced toward the house, eager to tell Mom all about it.

*****

"Layla! Are you awake? I am getting ready to leave for my first day of work."

Still half asleep, I squinted as my door opened.

Mom moved toward my bed, pulling her hair back into a bun. Still a little confused on how I made it to my room, I had no time to waste. I needed to tell Mom all about my adventure.

"Mom! Mom! You will never believe where I have been!" I suddenly shouted in excitement.

"Oh, wonderful, my love. Tell me all about where our next imaginary adventure will be when I get home. I can't be late for my first day of work."

"What do you mean?" I sat in confusion. "Aren't you just getting done work?"

"Sweetie, are you okay? You must have been in a deep sleep." Mom brushed her hand over my hair to free it from my face. I looked over to the wall and noticed there was no paint. I finally realized I must have been dreaming the entire time.

"Okay, Mom. Have a great day, I love you!"

Mom blew me a kiss as she walked back into the hallway to leave. I caught the kiss with my hand and waved goodbye. Lying back against my pillow, I couldn't stop thinking about my dream. Dad was looking over me, always would be.

I got myself together and decided to start my day with painting. As I struggled to open the paint lid, I thought about Dad. In my dream, he rushed to help me when I was in need. If only he was here, helping me open this paint can. I tried opening it with a screwdriver but failed, over and over again. The purple walls would have to wait until Mom got home. I decided to explore. I made my way outside and into the field. I, once again, was reminded of my dream. I kept hearing Dad say, *"With your adventurous side and your mother's imagination, you guys could really create something great there..."* The words swirled around in my head until they sparked a lightbulb to go off.

"I know exactly what we can do! We need to create the Sky of Bliss! Right here on the farm!"

CHAPTER 10
Inspired

My brain was spinning. I couldn't wait until Mom got home from work, but I was worried too. There is no way Mom will agree to this. She just started working. The house is still in horrible condition. I need to come up with a plan. Going to the kitchen, I grabbed a pen and paper and started to map out the Sky of Bliss. I wanted to recreate my dream.

"Roy the Rollercoaster! We could make the colorful carts ride along a rainbow!" I start drawing my visions on the paper, paying close attention to the details as I bit on my lower lip. It needed to be realistic. The rainbow needed to have beautiful hills and turns, to make the most fantastic ride.

Ray was so warm and welcoming... We could create a bright, lit up entranceway! It will be like you are walking through the sun. The pen hit the paper once again; I drew beams of light shooting from the tunnel entrance.

Liss loved to be joined by her fluffy friends! Instead of a trampoline area, we can create fluffy clouds to jump on. They will be soft but bouncy. I drew the clouds, and one after another, they spread for a mile long.

In honor of Dad, aka Gus, we could make a wind ride ... It can be a Windmill Ferris Wheel ride! It will move by big gusts of wind. Back to the drawing, I went. My lip now had an indentation from my teeth. The clock was ticking, and Mom would be returning home soon.

"I need to look at my canvas." Shoelaces dangling, barely tightened, I tripped as I raced out the back door, to look at the overgrown fields.

"Where do I start?" The farmland itself was in worse shape than the house.

"I need to label the fields." I went back inside and grabbed a marker. I then made my way to the fire pit as I grabbed half burnt pieces of wood from the ash. I labeled each ride on a separate piece of wood, then carried them around the farm.

The entrance to Ray was placed at the field that sat right against the road. Speed walking, I continued behind that field to a larger section that sat about a football field of a distance away. In this field, I placed a piece of wood that read, *Liss's Flufftastic Funasium.* A mile to the right of the clouds, would be the field for *Roy's Rainbow Rollercoaster.* I had one final log left to drop and the field that sat in the middle of the entire farm would be perfect.

"This field will definitely get the best wind flow. We can even set up large propellers to help." My imagination might have been taking over a little, but I knew Dad would be here to guide me and help this succeed.

From the constant running around, I took my shirt and wiped the sweat droplets off my forehead. The sun slowly lowered, and I knew the night was approaching. I couldn't believe how long I had spent on setting up my ideas. It had practically taken the entire day.

Screeeeeech! I quickly threw my hands over my ears to keep from hearing that awful, piercing noise. I noticed Mom pulling up to the house. Eager to share the news, I leaped forward.

"Mom! Mom!"

"Wow! Did someone miss me?" Mom looked exhausted but happy to see me.

"Yes, but I also have something exciting to tell you!" Out of breath, I started to explain my ideas. "And so if we had—"

"That is great," Mom interrupted, "but don't you want to know how your mother's first day of work went?"

I realized I should probably slow down, and so I stopped mid-explanation. I giggled and apologized. "How was your first day, Mom?"

"It was long but good. The people in this town are so friendly. I think this will be a good fit for us." Mom removed her shoes as she stretched her arms out. "Okay, so now what did you want to tell me?"

I couldn't compose myself. With all my excitement, I started to blurt out my ideas, "Dad came to me in a dream! I think we need to create the Sky of Bliss!"

"The Sky of Bliss? The place I told you sits above the clouds? The place that brings you happiness?" Mom's face filled with confusion.

I needed to explain more so she could understand. I needed her to believe in me. "Yes, but not in the sky, right here on the farm!"

"Oh, sweet girl. That sounds like a fantastic idea for one of our imaginary adventures."

I crossed my arms in frustration. "No. Mom, I mean it. We can create an amusement park that is inspired by the Sky of Bliss!"

Mom's smile quickly faded. I could feel her doubting me. She sat in silence for a minute as she shook her head. "Layla, it sounds wonderful, but there is no way we can do this. We can only use our savings for food and fixing up the house. I just started working, and only at minimum wage. We also don't know the first thing about building an actual amusement park."

I knew this would happen. I became so angered, I began shouting, "Dad believes in me!" I ran to the back of the house where I plopped down in the grass. As I yanked at the grass, a cool breeze tickled my neck. "Dad, I miss you," I sobbed. I felt bad for feeling angered, but I was upset. I felt so excited and it felt like that was all taken away. I missed Dad, I missed my friends, I just wanted something that could bring happiness back into my life.

"Layla!" Mom called after me as she ran to my side. "Layla, I believe in you too. I just don't know how we can pull this off. We need food to survive. And do you really want to live in an old, outdated house?"

I had no words. I felt defeated.

"So, what exactly did Dad say we need to do?"

I slowly lifted my head and wiped my face. "He said we need to use our imaginations."

Mom rubbed my back. "Well, that shouldn't be too hard. Any ideas you want to share?"

I jumped up, grabbed Mom's hand, and yanked her toward the front field. "I thought you'd never ask!" I beamed. "Okay, so, first, picture yourself walking through a sun! Bright lights! Beams shooting from a yellow tunnel! The warmest welcoming sign!" I pointed down at the log that read, *Ray's Warmest Welcome*.

"Amazing! Show me more!" Mom yelled out in excitement.

"Next, we have *Liss's Flufftastic Funasium*! We will have our guests jump from one fluffy cloud to the next. The clouds will lead them to other parts of the park." I continued to walk Mom through the fields, thinking on different features the park could have. "We have now reached *Roy's Rainbow Rollercoaster*. The rollercoaster will follow a twisty rainbow! It will be so much fun!"

Mom started running from field to field with me. I could tell she was excited, but something still seemed off. Her energy matched mine, but her face still showed concern. "*Gus's Windmill.* What is this going to be?" Mom read the final log.

"This is going to be a rideable windmill! With the wind and some propeller help, this will be the ultimate Ferris Wheel experience." I looked to Mom for her final reaction. My stomach tossed and turned. I wanted her approval so badly.

"I think this is stupendous! But—"

"But what?" My hands clammed up. I feared Mom's disapproval.

Mom's worried look disappeared as she smiled. "We need an ice cream mountain! We can start with a trail through sunflowers that leads up a mountain! Then everyone can decorate their own ice cream sundaes!" Mom placed her arm around my shoulder. "We need some sort of water ride too. That way, we can add all of our imaginary adventures."

I couldn't believe it. Mom agreed to my idea. She even seemed just as excited as I was. With both of our ideas, this would turn into the world's greatest amusement park.

"Forget the house being fixed. Your happiness means more to me than living in a perfect home. As long as we have a roof over our heads, we will be just fine. Let's start gathering ideas and head into town for some help."

I felt so grateful. It was not only time to get my happiness back, but we were about to spread it to everyone.

CHAPTER 11
Hopeful

We can't struggle anymore. Layla needs stability. She needs happiness. Henry, if you can hear me, please know I miss you more every single day. I do believe that you came to Layla in her dream. You were always there for her when she needed you the most. Just know that we will both need your guidance more than ever. I am scared but hopeful."

Mom was on the front porch when I overheard her talking to the sky. She had left the window cracked open, as I stood on the other side of the door, listening in. I had hoped this plan would work out, but I also didn't want to be a burden. If this failed, it would take years to fix up the house. Mom didn't deserve that.

Mom made her way over to the car. *Beeeeeep.* She laid on the horn. I waited a few seconds before opening the front door. I didn't want her to know I had been there the whole time.

"Come on, sweetheart! We need to make our way into town."

I skipped my way over to the car. "Mom, are you sure?"

"Sure about what?"

"About this crazy idea of mine. What if it costs too much? What if we fail?" I dropped my head, doubting everything. "I don't want to put more stress on you."

Mom gently tilted my head up as she placed her hand under my chin. "I have thought long and hard about this. It is not going to be easy. But I promise you, we will make it happen. And if it fails, at least we will have had fun trying. I have a good feeling about this. Dad would have wanted this. I know he will be with us, helping along the way."

I threw my arms around Mom, hugging her tightly. She was the strongest person I knew. I felt so lucky to have her as my mom. "To town we go." I smiled.

After four short minutes of a bumpy ride, we pulled up at The Rooster Café.

"Well, good evening, y'all. So happy to see your faces again," Nancy greeted us.

We placed our order and started jotting down ideas on the napkins. We wrote down the supplies we would need to get started. We also wrote down the names of the rides and entertainment.

"What are y'all brainstorming over here?" Nancy smiled. Everybody in town knew everybody's business. If they didn't, they were sure to find out.

"Call us crazy, but we want to transform the farm," responded Mom.

"Oh, how wonderful! Your great-grandmom would be so proud! So what fruits and veggies are you thinking?" Nancy was quick to make assumptions, but I couldn't blame her. That was what a farm was meant for.

"Oh no, we are creating an amusement park!" I couldn't hold back my excitement. I would shout it off the mountain tops if I could.

"Amusement park? Around these neck of the woods?" Nancy looked extremely confused.

"Well, yes. We are going to try our best. We don't know the first thing about the equipment we will need, but we are willing to learn." Mom tried to show enthusiasm but was beginning to look worried.

I rushed to explain, hoping to ease Mom's mind once again. "Dad passed away several months ago. We had to move here and are barely getting by. He came to me last night, in a dream, that is. He told me we needed to create something with our imaginations; so here we are."

"We are getting by just fine," Mom tried to reassure Nancy.

"You both are so brave. I admire your imagination. I know this town would help y'all out. We are here when someone is in need, and I reckon you both are in need more than anyone else here."

"We beyond appreciate it, but there is no need. We will figure it out, one way or another." Mom's cheeks flushed.

"Don't be silly. I am getting on the phone now and you will soon have some talented people showing up at your property."

I jumped out of the booth and squeezed her. My hope grew and I was ready to make my vision come to life.

"We thank you from the bottom of our hearts. Free admission when our gates open." Mom giggled as she, too, hugged Nancy.

Mom and I headed back home and waited for the help to arrive. We sat on the stoop and looked towards the narrow dirt road. One hour went by. *Is anyone going to show? They probably think we are nuts!*

"Do you really think people are coming?" I started to get nervous.

"Nancy seems true to her word. We just need to be patient."

Mom and I decided to play cards, to pass the time.

"A royal flush," Mom smirked as she laid her cards down. She had a tendency to always beat me at poker.

Another hour went by.

I was eager for the people to show up so we could get started. I started doing cartwheels in the grass. One after another, I started to get dizzy.

"Look!" Mom yelled as she pointed at the road.

I was still seeing double, from the constant flipping around. As I focused in, I could see dirt kicking up about fifty feet away.

"Is it them?"

"I'm not sure," responded Mom.

Honk, honk! A very loud horn blew, and a huge shipping truck made its way toward the house, but that wasn't the only truck. Another large one followed, and then another, and then another. Mom and I looked at each other in amazement.

The first truck pulled up and the driver leaned out his open window. "Hi, ma'am. We are here to help clear out these fields."

Mom seemed at a loss for words.

"Wow, mister! You are the best! You can start right over here. We need all of this cut down." I led the truck to each labeled area.

The next truck pulled up and the driver grinned. "Hey, y'all! I heard you need a really big and bold sign out here."

Mom stammered over her words, "Y-yes. If you c-can have it read *Sky of Bliss*. I thank you so much!"

The next truck made its way over. "We are here to build some amusement rides," the driver declared.

I stepped forward and cheered. It was really happening. "You are at the right place! So we will need a rollercoaster, a Ferris Wheel that looks like a windmill, bouncy clouds, a water ride, a space station, and a mountain, and..." I went on and on.

"I'd better be the first to try out the rides!" the truck driver said after I finally stopped talking.

"If you can create these rides, you will be the first and get free admission for a year!" I immediately responded.

Mom and the trucker both laughed together.

Men piled out of each truck and began tearing down the weeds and restoring the property. Mom and I delegated the tasks but also joined them to help out.

"Can you believe this, Mom?"

"The people in this town have exceeded all of my expectations. This has me feeling very grateful and optimistic," she said with a smile.

"I love you." I grabbed Mom's hand. I wanted her to know how grateful I was for her.

"I love you more."

After three hours of hard work, the sun started to set. Mom and I thanked all of the workers. Mom sent them each home with a jug of her homemade lemonade. She also gave them containers of oatmeal cookies.

"We will see you tomorrow." She waved them off.

"Mom, today has been the first day since Dad passed that I have actually felt excitement." I let out a heavy sigh, before smiling at the cracked ceiling above me.

"Sweetheart, I feel the same way. I am supposed to head into work tomorrow. So, let's get a good night's rest."

"Mom, you can't work. We have too much to do around here." I worried I wouldn't be able to handle this on my own.

"I know, sweetie. I will try to arrange my schedule to make this all work." She blew me a kiss, and I quickly caught it.

"Mom, you are doing the best job."

She smiled as her tired eyes slowly closed.

The sun shone brightly through the windows. I wiped my tired eyes and made my way to the window. I peered out over the cut-down fields. My heart felt so happy. Today was going to be great.

A smell filled our room. "*Mmm!* Bacon." I threw my blanket off and hurried down the stairs. "It smells amazing!"

"Well, I figured a full belly will help you get your day off to a great start." Mom dished eggs, bacon, and French toast onto my plate. "I am only working a half day today. I will be home around lunchtime, and I will then join the workers to get this park done."

Shortly after Mom left, all of the trucks returned and set off into the fields. I was determined to accomplish this goal and have everything done as quickly as possible. We had no time to waste.

Noon hit, and Mom pulled down the road. Covered in dirt, I was relieved to see her and excited to show her all the work that had been done.

She parked and made her way over to greet me, stopping in her tracks when she looked over the largest sign, reading, *Sky of Bliss*. She was instantly brought to tears. "It is beautiful."

"Do you love it?"

"Layla, this is more than my imagination could have dreamt up!" Mom hugged me. She jumped right in, helping the workers.

****

Weeks had gone by. Mom was working part-time at the Piggly Wiggly. She spent all of her other time helping the workers and me create a masterpiece.

"Hey, Mom! How was work?"

"Great. Went by fast today." Mom looked around the farm as her eyes lit up. "Wow, seems like the rides are almost all complete."

"Follow me! I want to show you the best part!" I grabbed Mom's hand as I pulled her through the fields.

"Let me guess, *Space Station*?"

I continued to pull Mom's hand, only stopping when I brought her to the very back of the park. Hundreds of stumps were scattered around the benches that were spread out. A sign read, *Dad's Bonfire*.

Mom's eyes paced back and forth as she noticed fire pits everywhere! There were also two food trucks set up with s'mores supplies inside. Mom took a seat on one of the benches. "Layla, this is perfect," she whispered. "Your dad would have loved this."

CHAPTER 12
Bliss

A
fter a few months of the entire town coming together, the park was almost complete—just like that! Mom wanted to give back to the people of town and show them support as well. We made our way to the diner and spoke to Nancy. We figured out a plan for the diner to supply all of the desserts at the amusement park. Then, we both headed over to the Piggly Wiggly, Mom's workplace.

"Hey there, Kristine. Isn't it your day off?" Kathleen smiled.

"Hi, Kathleen! I missed you too much." Mom giggled.

Kathleen laughed as well.

I decided to chime in, "We have a question for you."

Kathleen pulled me in for a hug. "Is that right? Anything for you."

"We need food to sell at the amusement park."

"Think you might want to supply it all?" Mom joined in.

Kathleen looked shocked. "Absolutely! We would love that! I promise you will have the freshest ingredients and the tastiest treats!"

Mom leaned over and hugged Kathleen. I wrapped my arms around them both. We thanked Kathleen once again, as we waved and made our way to the next stop, the local mechanic.

Feet stuck out from an old car.

"1959 Corvette, she is a beauty," Mom said.

It had a sparkly red exterior, with matching white and red leather interior. Mom always found the beauty in old cars. She and Dad would go to a classic car show every year. She would go on and on about all of the amazing cars and trucks. I don't even think Dad cared to see them. He would smile at Mom while she explained every detail of the classic cars. Her excitement made him happy.

"Excuse me. I don't mean to interrupt. Is there any way I can have a word with you?"

The feet slid forward. Blackened nails and oil on his shirt, the mechanic sat himself up. "Hey there. You are the one building that amusement park on the Cooper property, haven't seen you around before."

"Yes, that would be me."

"Pleasure to meet you. My name is Chris."

"This is my daughter Layla, and my name is Kristine."

"What can I help you ladies with?"

"We need a mechanic on stand-by, just in case any of the rides need fixing. Any chance you would want the job?"

Chris placed his wrench on the ground. He then rubbed his dirt-filled fingers on his shirt and extended his hand. "Ma'am, you have yourself a deal."

After a full day of running around, we were able to have the entire town involved in the park. We had food, drinks, a mechanic, extra workers, and an electrician. The sun started to set and the sky slowly turned a navy blue color.

"Hey, ma'am. We have everything completed. We wanted to show you one last thing." The general contractor motioned Mom and me to the front of the park where the big sign sat. He pointed to a small switch that sat closer to the ground. "Okay, little lady, you do the honors." He pointed to the switch again and smiled at me.

My hands became sweaty. My heart started to race. This was it. This would be the moment my dream would come to life in front of my eyes. I slowly bent down and flicked the switch. Huge bulbs lit up around the *Sky of Bliss* sign.

"Layla, look."

Turning, I took it all in. The entrance tunnel had beams of light shooting off in every direction and each section had a designated light. *Ray's Warmest Welcome* shone the brightest yellow. *Liss's Flufftastic Funasium* illuminated white. *Roy's Rainbow Rollercoaster,* of course, had rainbow-themed lights. *Gus's Windmill* shone almost as bright as the entrance tunnel, with a purple light. *Ice Cream Mountain* beamed a pale pink. *Space Station* was lit up with galactic green. *Under the Sea* had a sparkle of blue. *Treasure Island* radiated a beautiful orange. *Dad's Bonfire* was surrounded with stringed lights that added the perfect touch. Food trucks and game stations filled in all of the empty areas. The workers had even created a large parking lot, with glow-in-the-dark parking spots.

"I think the planet Pluto could spot this place." The contractor laughed while Mom and I stared.

We couldn't believe our eyes. We looked at one another, smiled, and embraced each other with the world's longest hug.

"You did it, Layla! This really does feel like a dream."

"No, Mom, *we* did it."

We continued our hug and yanked the contractor in for a group embrace. He dropped his clipboard and leaned in. This was going to be spectacular!

Word spread quickly to the towns surrounding Elkville, then those towns passed the word on to other towns. Word of mouth had people getting very excited. After a month of preparation, Sky of Bliss was ready to make its debut to the world. Mom and I kept busy that morning, making sure everything was perfect.

The noise of a loud truck made its way down the paved road, and I froze before shouting, "Mom! Mom! Dad's truck!"

"Hey there," the driver greeted as he parked in front of the house and got out. "Wow, this is something." He feasted his eyes on the park.

"You have no idea how much I missed this truck. Thank you!" Sending a smile to me, Mom continued, "Today is our opening day. Come back later, and I will treat you to some peach cobbler."

The driver licked his lips. "I wouldn't miss it! I will be bringing the whole family!" He got into the beaten down car and drove off.

"Well, at least we will have one customer," I joked.

The clock was ticking, and we were only a few short minutes from opening. The entire town of Elkville had arrived. Either they were working the park or were here to show support and have the time of their lives!

Mom and I stood at the entrance, thanking every single guest as they entered. Ten turned into twenty, twenty turned into thirty, thirty turned into almost one-hundred people! Mom and I were shocked at the turn out.

"Layla!!!!" Savannah and Johnny ran up and jumped on me. Then the rest of the old neighborhood made their way over.

I couldn't believe it. I started to cry happy tears. "What are you doing here?"

"Your mom called us and told us all about your amazing idea! We wouldn't miss this for anything." Savannah hugged me once again.

Already feeling overwhelmed, I then saw Gram walking up. My tears really started to come down.

"My girls! I am so very proud! And for you, Layla, here is a special treat." Gram handed me a shirt that read, *Creator of the Sky Of Bliss*.

"You are the best!" I threw it over the top of my rainbow dress.

Mom hugged Gram. I could tell Mom needed her here just as much as I did. As Mom caught Gram up on all of the excitement, I ran around with my friends. I showed them how each ride was inspired by our adventures. As the day progressed, I joined Mom. We made our way around to the workers, thanking them, and offering a hand.

A man, dressed in a fancy suit, made his way toward us. "Hi there. You must be Kristine and Layla."

I nodded my head.

"Welcome to the Sky of Bliss." Mom smiled.

The man held a briefcase as he reached inside to pull out a thick folder. "My name is Richard. I am the head director for Amusement Park Enterprises. I heard through the grapevine that a pretty magical place was opening in one of the smallest towns. I had to come take a look for myself."

"Wow, it is so nice to meet you. Thank you very much for traveling here. Let us show you around."

Richard followed us around to every part of the park. His face lit up every time I spoke of each ride and activity. "You don't see many people nowadays like Walt Disney. He had an eye for magic. He had an eye for fun. His imagination was like no-one else's. But today, I have been shown a place like no other. You remind me a lot of him. The Sky of Bliss is exceptional. I commend you both. I would love nothing more than to offer you a contract to be a permanent chain of Amusement Park Enterprises. I want to put this place on the map! Children around the world need to experience this."

Mom was at a loss for words. I became at a loss for words.

"I know today is your opening day, so I will leave this paperwork with you, and I hope we can discuss our future plans."

"I truly don't have words. This is an honor. I will go over the paperwork and reach out as soon as I have it all completed. Thank you! Thank you! Thank you!" Mom looked down at me and winked.

Richard smiled and stuck out his hand, but before Mom could shake it, I hugged him instead. Mom and Richard both laughed.

"I look forward to hearing from you both."

Mom and I looked around at children's smiling faces, parents joining in on the fun, and the town's people staying busy. This was what it was all about.

"Mom! This is like the best day ever!"

"It sure is."

"Can you believe it! Amusement Park Enterprises! Are you kidding me? This is the coolest thing ever!" I jumped up and down. With excitement taking control of my body, my arm knocked into the bundle of balloons tied to the sign. They became unraveled and started to float along the grass. "Oh no! I'll get them!" I started to chase after them as they quickly floated through the park and into the back field that sat beside the bonfire. Just as I grabbed the string, I noticed something sitting in the field.

Is that a basket? I walked over to see the exact basket from my dream. I looked down and noticed a piece of paper inside.

Hey, squirt. It's me... Dad. You really did it. The Sky of Bliss is out of this world! I am so proud of you. Remember, I will be by your side guiding you every day. Also know, your happiness will never go away as long as you create it from inside of you.

Tell your mom I love her.

I love you forever and always.

As soon as I read the last line, a large gust of wind whipped around me. "I love you too, Dad."

I skipped back to Mom. She was laughing with Gram and a few people from the old neighborhood. I skimmed the park as I saw my friends bouncing around with excitement. People from town came up, congratulating us.

I grabbed onto Mom's hand. She leaned down and kissed my head. In that moment, I felt pure bliss.

The End

ABOUT THE AUTHOR

Author Alicia Fadgen, from an early age, was inspired to bring joy to children. Her first jobs consisted of babysitting and working at a toy store. Now, as a mother, she strives to create imagination and a love of reading through her magical stories. Alicia currently resides in New Jersey with her husband, 3 children, and dog.

Made in the USA
Middletown, DE
06 December 2022

17245569R00076